"Reba, did you wake me up?"

Jase's deep voice was thick with slumber.

She drew in a sleepy breath. "No."

"I must have been dreaming, then."

He didn't say more, and after a long moment Reba rolled over in bed and looked at him. His eyes were closed as if he'd fallen back asleep. "Dreaming about what?" she asked, now fully awake and intrigued.

He mumbled something unintelligible, but then she noticed a muscle twitching in his jaw. She rose on her elbow, peered down at his face and made a bold guess. "It must have been sex." When his eyelids flew open, she exclaimed, "Aha! I thought so."

All trace of sleepiness vanished, and his mouth curved into a teasing, sensual smile. "How did you guess?" He pulled her partly on top of him. "I was dreaming about this dark-haired, dark-eyed woman. A wild, wanton creature . . . insatiable, really." He stared at the ceiling, apparently preoccupied with his fantasy.

"Anyone you know?"

"Yes, actually. I *do* know her . . . intimately."

Nancy Morgan and **Kate Fleming**, the two halves of writing team Jenny McGuire, have had diversified careers. Kate has been a counselor, teacher, researcher and flight attendant, as well as raising four children with her husband of thirty-one years. Nancy was in real estate before running an antique store and remains happily single. Despite their different backgrounds and life-styles, both women decided they love to write and made the move to romance writing. We're certainly glad they did.

Nancy and Kate live only a few blocks from each other in Seattle, Washington, which helped immensely while they were working together on *Christmas Wishes*, their first Temptation.

Christmas Wishes

JENNY McGUIRE

Harlequin Books

TORONTO • NEW YORK • LONDON
AMSTERDAM • PARIS • SYDNEY • HAMBURG
STOCKHOLM • ATHENS • TOKYO • MILAN

Our thanks to Pat Heagle, Sheila Slattery
and Selwyn Marie Young, members
of our original romance writers critique group.
Their help and belief in us
contributed to the success of this book.

Published December 1988

ISBN 0-373-25332-X

Prologue

HUNT'S POINT. Lakeside estates for some of Seattle's most rich and famous. Reba McCallister hesitated before turning her old Volkswagen bug into the wooded peninsula. For two weeks she'd fought the temptation to come here, and doubts still nagged at the back of her mind.

Nearing the Kingsford estate, she found the property almost obscured by dense evergreens and leafy vine maples, scarlet in the September sun. A wrought-iron gate secured the driveway, and beyond she could see only the five white dormers of a large house that sat down close to the water. She headed to the end of the road, turned the car around and shifted into park to wait. She hated sneaking around like this but knew she had no other choice.

Every minute that dragged by put her more on edge, making it torture to sit still. She pushed her unruly cocoa-brown curls away from her face. Her shoulders felt kinked and her slim legs cramped. She used to think her average frame fit neatly into her compact car, but now in her tense state she felt about to burst out of the confining space. Needing something to occupy her, she reached for the newspaper society page that had begun this quest.

She'd often read the local, suburban paper in the nurses' lounge when she took a break from her emergency-room duties. Like most people she took vicarious pleasure at viewing candid photographs of the local high society and reading juicy bits of gossip. This time a photographer must have approached the Kingsford house from the water side and used a telephoto lens. The close-up shot showed a young girl smiling as she opened a large gift-wrapped box. Reba scanned the caption.

No boys or adults allowed. That seemed to be the theme of Becky Kingsford's twelfth birthday party, celebrated by a bevy of young beauties on the balloon- and flower-festooned lawn of the family's million-dollar estate. Becky is the adopted daughter of *Seattle Examiner* owner-editor Jason Kingsford. Becky's adoptive mother, Carolyn Kingsford, a leader in Seattle society events, died a year ago.

For the hundredth time Reba studied the photograph, examining every detail of Becky Kingsford's face: her determined square jaw, wavy fair hair, almond-shaped light-colored eyes. It was uncanny! Every feature appeared to have skipped a generation. The photo might have been of Reba's mother as a young girl.

Movement ahead attracted Reba's attention. The wrought-iron gates were being opened electronically, and out of the driveway came an olive-green Bronco with a sandy-haired, broad-shouldered man at the wheel and a blond girl at his side.

She was in luck! It must be Jason Kingsford and his daughter, Becky.

Reba's palms became damp with nervous perspiration as she followed them out of Hunt's Point. It took every ounce of discipline she possessed to keep well back as he drove onto the freeway, then off again to enter a residential area some miles east. Tailing turned out to be harder than she'd expected, and she swore as a moving van swung in front and blocked her view. She caught sight of the Bronco again just as it turned through twin brick gateposts, above which arched a sign reading Forest Park Stables. It was a beautiful place, with several barns and riding rings tucked into the fir- and cedar-wooded acres of a huge suburban park.

Jason Kingsford finally brought the truck to a halt in front of a red-brick building complete with a clock tower. Reba had just found a spot to park in the crowded lot when she saw Becky hop out of the Bronco, a bulky canvas tote bag slung over one shoulder. Her fashionable jeans hugged slender legs, and her long honey-colored curls bounced against her red sweater as she sprinted toward the indoor riding arena. Reba knew she should just turn around and leave before this got even more out of hand. But as soon as Jason Kingsford drove away, she found herself heading after Becky.

Inside, Reba halted in the wood-floored aisle that separated the tiers of bleachers from the arena fence and let her eyes adjust to the dimmer light of the cavernous interior. The pleasant, earthy aroma of horses filled her nostrils. Hearing a woman's bellowed command to mount up, Reba looked over to see a stern-faced instructor assembling a group of youngsters for an English-style riding lesson. Becky was nowhere to be seen, but Reba suspected it was this lesson she'd been running to. Perching on the bottom bleacher, Reba waited anxiously for the blond girl to appear.

It didn't take long for her hunch to pay off. Becky, now wearing canary breeches and knee-high black riding boots, came jogging down the aisle toward her. As she approached, her gait slowed to a limping hop-step.

"Oh, great! And I'm late already!" With a sigh of frustration she sank down next to Reba and began struggling to remove one of her boots.

"Can I help?" Reba asked, hoping the thumping of her heart wasn't loud enough to be heard.

Becky looked up, and Reba's breath caught in her throat. There in the girl's right eye was a brown spot in the blue cornea identical to the one Reba's mother had possessed. The rare hereditary trait was the final, conclusive evidence.

This was her child!

Becky grimaced, her slightly upturned nose wrinkling as she gave the boot another futile tug. "I have something in my boot, and these dumb things are too small for me. I can get them on myself, but someone always has to help me get them back off."

"Hold your foot up here. I'll give it a try." Reeling inwardly from emotion, Reba reached for the boot with trembling hands. She'd been only sixteen when she'd signed the papers for Becky's adoption, and now she'd found the daughter she'd thought was lost to her forever. Joy surged in her chest. She wanted to shout in relief and celebration. She wanted to cry. Yet she knew she must do nothing of the kind. *Get hold of yourself*, she scolded. *You can't break down here.*

"You have to pull really hard," Becky said.

"Okay, here goes nothing." She waited until Becky had a good grip on the bleacher before yanking with all her might. The next thing Reba knew, she was flying backward. Then her bottom connected solidly with the hard floor and she gasped.

"Oh, no!" Becky scrambled to take the boot from Reba and give her a hand up. "They never come off that easily. Geez, I wish Dad would buy me some new ones. I'm so sorry, Mrs.—"

Reba plopped down on the bench, shaken, but not by the tumble. She wondered if this was all a dream from which she would soon wake. "My name's Reba. Reba McCallister."

Becky tipped the boot upside down to shake out the offending pebble. All at once Reba felt uncontrollable mirth bubble up from within. She chuckled. Then, as her pent-up anxiety and exultation released, she laughed. Becky started to laugh along with her, then caught the impatient glance of her riding instructor. She tightened her lips in an attempt to stifle her giggles, but as her impudent blue eyes met Reba's brown ones, she laughed out loud again. Their efforts to be serious only made the situation seem funnier. Becky's shoulders shook so hard she could barely get her boot back on. Finally ready, she jumped up. "Thanks, Reba." She started off, ran a short distance, then stopped and looked back. "My name's Becky. I hope I'll see you here again."

Becky joined the riders and took the reins of a snorting, sidestepping pinto. Mounting in a graceful motion, she began reining in tight circles until she had the powerful animal completely under her control. She fell into line with the others and, when the instructor turned her head, wiggled her fingers at Reba.

Reba gave a jaunty wave back. Tears threatened again, and in an attempt to regain control she squeezed her eyes shut. When she reopened them, she discovered Becky staring at her. *No, she's not looking at me*, Reba realized as an elderly man rode a chestnut mare toward her. It was the mare, with her spirited gait, who'd captured Becky's interest.

Halting at the fence where Reba stood, the man dismounted in slow motion, as though the effort was more than his old bones wanted to make. "Hand me that jacket there in the bleachers, would you?" he asked Reba, who complied by reaching for it.

The mare nosed her blouse in a friendly manner. Gently stroking the horse's wide blaze, Reba glanced at Becky, who was still watching intently.

"This little Arab filly's for sale," the man said, jerking her attention back to him. He studied her heart-shaped face, framed by soft waves like an old-fashioned heroine. "You look to me like a kind person. I'd like to see my Amber go to someone like you."

"Me? Buy this horse?" She laughed giddily, then shook her head, still so overwhelmed by the miracle of finding her daughter that she couldn't think straight.

"You like horses. I can see that," he said.

"I do. But I haven't had a chance to do much riding."

He gestured toward the riding class. "They have excellent instruction here."

Taking advantage of the opening, she ventured, "Becky Kingsford seems quite good."

"You know Becky?" he asked, his interest piqued. Reba's smile of confirmation was all the encouragement he needed to continue eagerly, "She's a great gal, isn't she? A dandy young horsewoman. Not a timid bone in her body. Has a real good seat and hands, too."

"She loves horses," Reba put in, hoping to keep him talking.

"Ha!" He snorted. "That's an understatement. She would live and breathe them if she could. Too bad about her father being the way he is."

"Uh-huh."

"Yep. If it were up to Becky, she'd be riding every day. She'd keep up her training and someday be one of the greats." A cloud seemed to pass over his craggy face, and he pursed his lips contemplatively. "This past year, though, well . . . her father's been keeping her pretty close to home. If you ask me, that one is courtin' trouble if he doesn't loosen up the reins."

Even though Becky appeared to be well cared for, the man's remarks filled Reba with uneasiness. As an adolescent, she had rebelled against her own overly strict father—with disastrous results.

"I just saw him leave," Reba said, continuing to fish for information. "He seemed in a hurry."

"He's a busy man, I suppose."

"A tyrant who's too busy for his daughter," Reba murmured, becoming more worried by the moment. As she tried to digest all that she'd learned, Reba stroked the mare's silky neck. Mistaking her thoughtfulness for interest in his horse, the man began to list the animal's good qualities. When he quoted his price, nearly what she'd saved to buy a much-needed new car, Reba found herself actually considering it. The desire to get to know her daughter and make certain of her happiness grew stronger with each passing moment. From what he'd said, she knew owning a horse would gain her access to Becky. Becoming a regular around the stable would make it easy for her to befriend Becky and learn about her life with Jason Kingsford. There would be no need to reveal her true identity and disturb Becky's world. In a month or so, if all proved well, she could slip out of her daughter's life again.

"She's a wonderful girl," the man was saying as he patted the mare. "If you ask me, you two were meant to be together."

Reba nodded, staring past the horse to her daughter. With a decision born more in her heart than in her head, she declared, "Sold."

1

REBA CROSSED the stable yard heading toward Amber's barn, golden autumn leaves crunching beneath her new riding boots as she walked briskly along. A warm late-afternoon breeze tossed her hair into her face, and she whisked back the dark brown curls, unconcerned. Everything was right with the world today because she knew that later she was bound to see Becky.

Leaving the bright October sunlight behind, Reba entered the barn, soaking up the sights and sounds and smells of horses as she made her way down the aisle. As a girl, she had been as horse-crazy as Becky was now, only without the means to pursue the interest. It seemed more than a whim of fate that mother and daughter shared this passion. Reba mused over the circumstances that had conspired to throw them together. She had never intended to seek out her child and break the agreement of confidentiality she had signed so long ago. But that newspaper photograph had been irresistible. She'd almost been able to hear Becky calling to her. It would have taken a person with a harder heart and stronger will than Reba's to resist the lure. And then at the stable two weeks ago there had been their incredible meeting, so much more wonderful than the fantasy reunions she'd imagined through the years. Their instant rapport had made Reba wonder if a primitive instinct had drawn her daughter to her.

From the first day a close friendship had developed between them, and Reba had to remind herself that she'd not sought out Becky simply to indulge her heart. Her mission was to determine Becky's state of well-being. What she'd learned did not ease her mind.

Though Becky's cheerful, extroverted nature made her a delight to be around, there was more going on inside than her sunny face let on. As they'd grown closer, Reba had encouraged confidences. Although Becky seldom spoke of her mother, she complained often about her father's strictness and overprotectiveness. What frightened Reba most was that Becky did more than moan; several times she'd acted out her frustration by blatantly disobeying him.

Reba could only speculate about Jason Kingsford, for she had yet to meet him. He never came to the stable, other than to drop Becky off. Besides the negative comments she'd heard about him, she knew only that he was rich and secure in Seattle's power structure as owner-editor of the *Examiner*, a newspaper held by the Kingsford family for three generations.

"Hi, sweetie," Reba cooed as she approached Amber's stall. The Arabian mare swung her blazed face around in greeting. Sliding open the heavy wooden stall door, Reba entered and placed her grooming box on the edge of the manger. She began brushing vigorously, taking pleasure in seeing Amber's coat gleam like a polished piece of the precious stone after which she'd been named. Reba had just begun humming contentedly when, above the din of the stable activities, she heard a masculine voice calling for Becky. The tune lodged in her throat, and she strained to hear. The unfamiliar voice, resounding with authority, caused goose bumps to rise on her skin.

Jason Kingsford. It must be him, she thought.

The sound of his voice grew louder as he came down the long length of the barn, stopping twice along the way to ask if anyone had seen his daughter. Most likely he would ask her, too. With the time to meet Becky's adoptive father finally at hand, Reba's mouth became dry with uncertainty. If only she'd given more careful consideration to how she would go about introducing herself to him. She'd thought she could simply wing it— act in whatever manner seemed appropriate at the time. But now, with Mr. Kingsford approaching, her mind stalled like the engine of the rattletrap car she was still forced to drive.

Her concentration on Becky's father instead of her work, Reba scrubbed mindlessly at Amber's hide until the distressed look in the horse's eyes brought her hands to a halt. This would never do. She knew it was imperative to act naturally, as though she were any other casual acquaintance of Becky's. Besides, there was no reason for her to be so nervous and fearful. No reason, she thought gloomily, except for her deep-rooted sense of guilt about her deception.

At the sound of his footfalls on the concrete aisle, she felt her stomach knot into a tight ball. He was only a stall away now. She dropped the brush onto the wood-shaving bedding where it bounced beneath Amber's back hooves. As she knelt and reached to retrieve it, she saw a pair of lean, denim-clad legs enter the doorway of the stall.

"Hello in there." His deep voice seemed to vibrate off the walls and into her very being. "I wonder if I might speak with you?"

Reba's chin jerked up. From her crouched position halfway under her horse, she looked up at the man in the doorway. She sat unmoving, surprised by her immediate impression of Jason Kingsford. Her preconceived notion of a newspaper editor was of someone skinny and pale. This man didn't look as though he spent much time hunched over typed pages. Instead, his rugged handsomeness suggested a love for the outdoors. His wind-tousled dark blond hair had the golden sheen of polished pine, as did the mustache above his firm unsmiling mouth. The sleeves of his maroon leather jacket were pushed up to expose tanned forearms, and the coat hung open to reveal a muscular chest. The unbuttoned V-neck of his black knit shirt drew her attention to the sensual hollow at the base of his throat, but her gaze was soon pulled to his deepwater blue eyes.

He observed her openly, unnerving her with his boldness. Finally releasing her gaze, he made a sweeping appraisal of her, as though forming an opinion then and there while she hovered beneath him. Reba rose stiff-leggedly, hoping she'd feel more confident when the difference between their heights measured inches instead of feet. But when she stood erect, he still looked down at her, at least six inches taller than her five foot five.

"I'm looking for my daughter," he announced. Lines of tension radiated from the corners of his eyes. "I believe you know her . . . Becky Kingsford."

For a brief moment panic swept through Reba, rendering her speechless. How did he know about her? But of course, Becky must have mentioned something.

Noticing her confusion, he asked, "You are Reba, aren't you?"

"Yes, yes, I am," she said in a rush, then took a deep breath to get a grip on herself. She forced her voice to sound casual as she added, "But I haven't seen Becky today. I recall her saying she would be at the horse show in the park, though. Have you looked there?"

"Not yet. I had hoped I would catch her here first."

Feeling calmer now, Reba studied him anew and found herself thinking what an attractive man he was. Handsome, indeed, and sexy, too. Her thoughts seemed to be sensed by him, for a knowing gleam came into his eyes. She turned and began brushing Amber's neck, but even with her back to him she felt his presence. There was something about Jason Kingsford that electrified the air. It made her so uncomfortable she wished he would leave—and yet she knew this was the opportunity she'd been waiting for. For her own peace of mind, she must make an effort to become better acquainted with him.

Keeping that resolution foremost in her mind, she tossed the brush into the grooming box and forced her mouth into a smile. In her friendliest voice she asked, "Hand me that saddle and pad sitting in the aisle, would you?"

Trying not to be obvious, she watched his smooth athletic movements as he bent to reach for the saddle. He lifted it as though it weighed nothing, then surprised her by entering the stall. He placed the sheepskin pad on Amber's back just behind her withers and smoothed the creases that might irritate the mare's skin. Then he topped the pad with the English saddle.

"That's the extent of my experience with horses," he said. "You'll have to do the rest."

"Thanks." She reached for the girth and pulled it up just snugly enough to keep the saddle secure. "I take it that you're not as keen on horses as Becky is."

"You're right. I'm not. Look, I'm pretty sure if Becky is on the premises, she'll find her way to you."

Again Reba suffered a pang of guilt. "Why do you think she'd come see me?"

"Your horse here. Becky was after me to buy this mare for her."

Reba recalled the anger and disappointment in Becky's eyes when she'd said she'd discussed buying Amber with her father. It didn't take much reading between the lines to guess that they'd done more than politely talk it over.

She slipped on the snaffle bridle. "I didn't know when I bought Amber that someone else was interested in her. If you still want her . . ." She let the sentence dangle, hoping he would snap up her offer. She'd love to give her daughter the horse she wanted so much.

"Very generous of you. But unnecessary. I wouldn't have bought the mare for her, anyway." A sharp-eyed intelligence radiated from Jason Kingsford as he assessed the situation. "If Becky does come around today, I'd like to hear about it." He withdrew a wallet from the back pocket of his snug-fitting jeans and slipped out a business card. "You can reach me at this number."

Reba ignored the proffered card and began buckling the bridle's neck strap. She knew it wasn't prudent to challenge Becky's father, but she resented the position he was placing her in. Reporting on Becky would unravel the trust she'd so carefully begun to knit between them. She had no choice but to take a firm stand with him. "I'm afraid I can't do that."

"And why not?" He stiffened, squaring his shoulders, not a man used to defiance.

"First, because I'm leaving to ride over to watch the horse show." It was a true effort to look Jason Kingsford in the eye and oppose him. "Second, because I don't tattle on little girls to their fathers."

He slowly replaced the card in his wallet. When he looked up at her again, she saw that his expression had tightened. "Would you consent to passing on a message?"

She shrugged. "Certainly."

His eyes flashed, like lightning over a stormy sea. "You can tell her that if she doesn't get home immediately, she'll be grounded until the moon turns blue." Without another word he turned on his heel and strode out of the stall.

Reba watched, wide-eyed with dismay, as he disappeared down the aisle. More than ever she felt sympathy for Becky. Obviously Jason Kingsford expected to be obeyed without question. An uncompromising, stubborn man. Just like her own father, Reba thought with anger welling.

Still fuming, Reba rode Amber onto the park's trails where she put her heels to the mare's sides. In the shadows of hemlock and cedar and fir Amber galloped, her hooves barely seeming to touch the earth as she ran with long, sweeping strides. They were halfway to the horse show grounds before Reba regretfully drew back to a walk. She held the moderate pace through a more densely wooded area where the scent of evergreen trees hung heavy in the air, and Amber had completely cooled off by the time they emerged from the woods. Reba headed for the show grounds, which consisted of a wood-fenced ring, a small set of bleachers, an announcer's tower and a concession shed. Near the show ring a group of pleasure riders had stopped to watch, and Reba trotted over to join them.

She was just kicking her feet out of the stirrups to stretch her legs when she heard her name being called. Scanning the crowd, she saw Becky jogging toward her, waving and smiling. She looked so carefree and happy that Reba hated to bring bad tidings.

"I was beginning to think you weren't coming today," Becky said, beaming up at Reba. She rubbed Amber's wide blaze and murmured a horsey version of affectionate baby talk.

"And I'm wondering why you're here at all," Reba rejoined, drinking in the sight of her daughter. Her blond springy hair, the texture so similar to Reba's, curled around her face and spilled over her shoulders. She looked polished and well-bred in her new designer jeans and bright yellow sweater. Becky's outfit was so different from the grubby things Reba had liked to wear at twelve.

Becky's forehead knit in perplexity. "I don't understand."

"I met your father at the stable and got the distinct impression that you're supposed to be at home right now."

The spark in Becky's eyes extinguished, and her body slumped as though her troubles weighed like pounds on her shoulders. She hugged Amber's neck and pressed her face against the satiny chestnut coat. "Is he coming here to get me?"

"I'm afraid he's on his way now." Reba dismounted, slanting a discreet glance at Becky's face. Her daughter's expression held disappointment, tension and possibly repentance—but not fear. At least she wasn't afraid of her father's temper, Reba thought in relief. "By the way," she said, "how did you get here? Did someone give you a lift?"

"I rode the bus. I go everywhere on the bus. Once I rode it all the way to Snoqualmie Falls."

"Miss Independence. Just like me at your age."

"Dad's going to be mad at me for taking the bus without permission, too. He always wants to know where I am and what I'm doing every minute of the day."

It had been wrong for Becky to break her father's rules, and Reba felt she had to say something whether she wanted to or not. "I hope you don't make a habit of going behind his back. You'll catch a lot of trouble that way."

"If I had asked, he would have said no, and I would be home right now instead of watching the show." Becky grinned in challenge, evidently believing her logic flawless.

Becky exhibited so many shining qualities that Reba had never thought of her as a bad child. Good grades came easily for her, as did friends. She was smart and funny and loving. The problem was that she was also proud and headstrong—a combination that could drive any parent to tears. It was hard to imagine Becky's self-possessed father reduced to a fit of frustrated crying, but a sudden sympathy for the man flared in her breast.

She didn't envy the job of controlling Becky. "My father used to tell me I had more guts than brains," Reba said, grinning despite her attempt to give Becky a quelling look. "And that my misbehavior would catch up to me in the end."

"Did it?"

"Yes. Just like coming here today is going to catch up to you." Reba glanced at her serviceable watch. "I'd say in about five minutes."

Becky sighed, then cracked a brave smile. "You're lucky to be an adult. The life of a kid can be the pits." Action in the ring caught her eye. "Oh, look! They're starting my favorite event."

Becky pointed to a rider putting a black horse over a series of low jumps and explained to Reba that the event was a class for hunters. But as Becky talked, her gaze roamed the show grounds, crowded with milling horses and riders.

"Are you trying to locate someone?" Reba asked. "Or just on the lookout for your father?"

"My friend Heather is competing in the next class and I'd better go tell her I'm not going to be here to watch her after all." Disappointment fell on Becky's face again. "It's the last show of the season—but Dad doesn't care about that at all."

In an effort to brighten her daughter's day, Reba said, "I'll tell you what. Why don't you take Amber and ride over to find Heather?"

"Oh, could I? I can't wait to see her face when I ride up on Amber!"

Reba waved her off, then leaned her elbows on the fence to watch the jumping. But it was Jason Kingsford, not horses, that was on her mind.

JASE MADE HIS WAY toward the horse show, heading first for the bleachers. When a round of jumping ended, the audience exploded into exuberant applause, reverberating in the cool air like the excited bursts of chatter in the newsroom whenever one of his reporters returned from the field with a hot story. Well, he had a news bulletin for Becky when he found her: her lies were going to stop.

After searching the bleachers for Becky without success, he headed for a group of riders not far away at the show-ring fence. As he approached them, he saw the gently curved figure he recognized as the spirited woman from the stable.

Almost the instant his gaze touched her, her spine arched like an angry cat's.

"Well, hello again, Mr. Kingsford," she said in tight-lipped greeting. Her large dark brown eyes, which he'd found so disturbingly intense, impaled him once again. She lifted her chin and held up a leather-gloved hand. "Before you ask—yes, I have seen Becky."

"I hope you told her I was looking for her." He tried to keep the irritation from his voice, but his temper was strained.

"She got your message, although it was an edited version."

He realized he wouldn't locate Becky any faster by charging through the grounds like an outraged parent and decided it was about time to exhibit some of the restraint he usually prided himself on mastering. "I didn't mean to take it out on you, Miss..."

"McCallister."

"Reba McCallister." He put out his hand to shake hers. Though she hadn't removed her riding gloves, the leather couldn't completely disguise her pliant flesh.

Hastily she withdrew her hand. "Well, Mr. Kingsford—"

"Call me Jase," he corrected. Though uncertain why he cared, he felt a strong need to erase her unpleasant first impression of him. "Mr. Kingsford is reserved for employees and enemies. Jason was last used by a third-grade teacher who reprimanded me with a swat of a ruler on my hand. Everyone I care about calls me Jase."

"Jase," she repeated cautiously, as though trying his name on her tongue.

Jase took a moment to study her face, its boundaries softly blurred by a mass of dark curls. Her delicate and pretty features were as beguiling as those of Gibson girls he'd seen in the collection of old magazines inherited from his father. Mathias Kingsford would have been shocked at his granddaughter's outlandish behavior, Jase thought, knowing his father had tolerated no disobedience from him or his brother. "I came on too strong in the barn," he said. "Becky's the one I'm angry with."

Reba curtly nodded her acceptance of his apology. "Becky's a spirited girl. I imagine she tries your patience at times."

"That's an understatement."

"Did something happen?"

Normally Jase would not have discussed his daughter with a woman he barely knew. But Becky had mentioned her new friend Reba so often that she didn't seem like a stranger anymore.

Finally it was the concern in her eyes that made him decide to confide in her. "She's on restriction," he said. "Or she was supposed to be. I think she must have a secret tunnel out of the house. It didn't take much sleuthing to figure where she'd be headed, though. She has a severe case of horse fever." He braced a hand on the rough fence rail and glanced down at the hoof-marked soil. The turn of his thoughts caused a sharp pain to shoot through his stomach. Ever since Carolyn's death he'd been terrified that something would happen to Becky. His anxiety was unreasonable; he knew that. But logic didn't stop the fear. He released a puff of breath, frustrated by his lack of control over his emotions and his daughter. "Quite frankly, sometimes I wish I could simply lock her in her room and not let her out until she's twenty-one."

Reba's eyes opened wide. "I'm sure you don't mean that, Mr. Kingsford."

"No. I wasn't serious." He snorted and smiled ruefully. "It is a thought, however."

Reba picked at a splinter on the fence, thoroughly confused by her feelings about Jase Kingsford. Her fury with him had mysteriously evaporated when he'd taken her hand in his, and now she found herself wondering if she'd misjudged him. She noted his thick sandy lashes that were just a little lighter than his mustache, and her gaze traced the firm yet sensual line of his mouth. The one thing she knew for certain was that he possessed a quality that she seemed inordinately susceptible to.

The loudspeaker barked an announcement of the next round of competition, thankfully distracting her attention.

Jase nodded at the first girl entering the ring. "Becky's friend Heather," he explained. "I know Becky wanted to watch her perform today. I'd better go find her now, or she'll be getting her way."

On impulse, Reba touched his arm lightly. She felt his hard biceps through the leather. "Would that be so terrible? She'll only be twelve once."

"Old enough to behave."

"And young enough to still be a child," she countered.

"Well, this child has a lesson to learn."

Reba couldn't help but champion her daughter's cause. "There won't be many more warm, sunny days like this. Why not let her have a few more minutes of fun?"

"I suppose," he began slowly, "it would be easier to find her after this event is over. I wouldn't put it past her to be hiding out somewhere, and I'd look pretty ridiculous crawling under the bleachers searching for her."

"Good," Reba said simply. She grinned, and when he responded in kind, she couldn't help staring. The grimness in his face vanished, making him look years younger. "Could I ask just what crime Becky committed?" she asked.

He stopped smiling, and his jaw seemed to firm by reflex. "She lied. I won't tolerate that."

"Oh, but most kids fib occasionally." Reba couldn't comprehend his extreme anger. "Is that a capital offense in your home?"

"It's a pretty damn serious one. Especially when it becomes a habit." His blue eyes became as cold and unyielding as ice. "You probably know I'm a newspaperman. Credibility is the lifeblood of a journalist. My father brought me up to have a healthy respect for the truth. It's vital. Becky needs to learn that, too."

Reba remembered the masthead of the paper. Truth Above All. Jase might be overreacting to childish fibs, but she had to admire a man so committed to his principles.

He continued, "So you see, it wasn't the streaking alone that concerned me—"

His announcement so startled her that she could only laugh out an astounded, "What?"

"Streaking. As in dashing across the road with no clothes on. Becky was having a slumber party. The girls were sleeping out on the lawn. Or supposed to be sleeping. It seems they were daring each other to run across the road from Heather's driveway to ours—stark naked. Becky's turn came just when a police car began its patrol. The girls dared her to run. She did and got caught. The patrolman brought her home."

Reba snapped her mouth closed when she realized it had been gaping. "No wonder you were upset!"

"Actually, I was out that night. Becky lied to Ingrid, our housekeeper. She said she'd explained everything to me and that I didn't want the subject brought up. I didn't find out until yesterday. I grounded her for two months." At Reba's look of disbelief a frown furrowed his forehead. "Perhaps that's excessive. But she will be punished for her lies."

Despite the angry set of Jase's face, the prank was beginning to sound funny to Reba. "Can you picture that ride in the patrol car? Oh, dear! I have a feeling you won't have to worry about it happening again." Unable to restrain herself, she began to laugh.

Jase felt some of his tension wash away. He liked Reba's laughter, as unforced and spontaneous as a child's. She turned her attention to the show ring, and Jase found his gaze roaming her figure. She was no Gibson girl in that respect. Her shape was much more subtle. Still, her hips had a definite curve—not too much, but very feminine. Her breasts were in perfect proportion, he decided, feeling the stirrings of physical response. Perhaps more than her body, it was the mysterious quality about her that captivated him.

His thoughts were punctuated by a firecracker going off somewhere on the show grounds, probably lit by children enjoying some Fourth of July leftovers. Another firecracker exploded, causing a horse to shy and lunge sideways toward Reba. Jase yanked her to him and out of the way. Even after the rider regained control and urged his horse onward, Jase continued to hold her in his arms. She yielded to his grip, and as her breasts molded to his chest, his heartbeat accelerated.

Reba looked up into Jase's eyes. The storm she had seen there earlier had passed, the liquid blue now warm and inviting. The sensation of being slowly drawn into their current frightened her, yet at the same time she felt a thrill course through her body.

"Please," she said in a breathy whisper. "Let me go now."

Jase saw so much anxiety in her eyes that he released her at once. She stepped back, away from him.

Alarmed cries from across the arena drew his attention from her, his news-hound instincts springing to life. Climbing onto the fence, he tried to see above the dense, shifting crowd. The action in the ring came to an abrupt halt, and he pinpointed the disturbance in the concession area. There a horse was rearing, its mane and tail banners of red and its forelegs flailing the air above the heads of shrieking people. He couldn't see exactly what was happening, but a sickening feeling of dread worked at his stomach. He shaded his eyes with his hand, trying to get a better look. The horse reared again and turned its white-blazed face toward Jase.

It was Reba's horse, Amber. The one Becky had wanted.

He swallowed the hard lump in his throat and looked down at her. "Where's Becky?"

"Why?" Reba jumped up on the rail beside him, clutching his arm for balance. Seeing Amber's empty saddle, she stifled a cry. "Oh, my God, no!" Her frantic gaze flew to Jase. "I let Becky ride Amber."

Without another word she leaped from the fence into the throng. Suppressing his panic as much as he could, Jase raced after her, pushing his way through the confused mass of people and animals. He heard Reba demanding the right to pass and her assertion that she was a nurse. By the time he caught up to her, she was already on the ground, kneeling beside the still form of his daughter.

2

"YOUR COFFEE'S COLD." Reba watched Jase wake with a start, prop himself up on the waiting-room couch and grope for the Styrofoam cup on the table beside him. Bleary, he overshot his mark and sloshed the liquid onto his fingers.

"Damn!" He shook the coffee from his hand and glanced around the room, empty except for the two of them. He squinted at his watch, then at Reba, who now wore her nurse's uniform. "Good Lord, it's past three in the morning."

She handed him a fresh cup of steaming black coffee. "Here, drink this. It'll help you drive home."

"Thanks." He accepted her offering absently.

The lines of fatigue etched around his eyes spoke of the toll worry had taken on him. His suffering touched an emotion within her that she couldn't honestly pass off as natural concern for the well-being of others. "How long have you been asleep in here?" she asked.

"A couple of hours, I guess. I would have stayed with Becky, but I was afraid of falling asleep in the chair by her bed. I snore when I sleep sitting up. I didn't want to wake her."

"There's no need for you to sit here all night," she said firmly. "You know Becky's going to be fine. The doctor assured you her concussion was mild. She's only staying overnight for observation."

He leaned forward and braced his elbows against his knees. He cradled the cup in both hands, and there was a slight ripple in the coffee. "You don't know how scared I was when I saw Becky lying on the ground. All I could think of was—" His voice cracked and he drew in a ragged breath. "I thought . . ."

Jase's display of emotion melted the starch from Reba's knees, and she sank down at his side. "I know," she whispered, longing to tell him she had felt the same fear, a parent's fear. But she dared not reveal her identity. If he knew who she was, he would surely forbid her to see Becky again. Like any adoptive parent, he would be afraid his child's natural mother would try to claim her. "Jase, why don't you go home and get some sleep?" she implored. "Tomorrow you'll be glad you did."

"Oh, hell, you're probably right. I'm not accomplishing anything here." He rotated his shoulders as if to rid them of kinks. "Except to age by the minute."

He set the coffee down and then, reaching for her hand, rose and gently pulled her up to stand beside him. Keenly aware of the sensations his warm, strong grip sent spiraling up her arm, she withdrew her hand with a jerky motion. "I'd better get back to work," she said, restoring an impersonal quality to her voice.

He slung his leather jacket over his shoulder, giving her a sidelong glance at the same time. "Becky asked for you earlier."

"Oh? She was probably worried about Amber."

"Becky likes you very much. I appreciate the interest you've taken in her, but I have to tell you that I don't like what happened at the show grounds. I intend to see that nothing like it happens again." His ominous tone left little doubt he meant what he said. He continued in the same brusque manner. "You have to under-stand—"

Reba broke in. "I understand that it's been a long, difficult day and we're both on edge. Why don't we just say good-night at this point and save the discussion for another time?" She curled her nails into her palms as she struggled to meet his gave without flinching.

At last he tipped his chin in a slow nod. He headed for the door, but before leaving caught her eye. "I *will* see you tomorrow. Then we can discuss why Becky was riding your half-trained horse."

REBA STOOD behind the counter of the nurses' station, trying to suppress a yawn as she checked a patient's chart. Debbie Simpson, the flamboyant little redhead who had been her closest friend since they'd both be-gun working at Eastside General Hospital four years earlier, studied Reba with kohl-rimmed eyes. "You look beat, Reba. These twelve-hour shifts can be gruesome. Take a break. I'll cover for you."

Reba cast a tired glance at her watch. Nine in the morning. She loved being a nurse, but could do with-out the long hours, and the night and weekend shifts. "Maybe I should. This place has been a madhouse to-night. What a night to be shorthanded! I can't believe things have finally slowed down around here."

"On your way out, drop this in the mail slot, will you?" Debbie handed her an envelope.

"*Bride's* magazine. Does this mean Dr. Bob Button-Down Burton has actually proposed?"

Debbie tossed her fiery hair and grinned. "He will. I'm definitely planning on Bob taking me away from all this."

Reba smiled back and saluted Debbie with the envelope as she left. She hoped Debbie got her way. As far as Reba was concerned, she liked the excitement of the emergency room and the extra responsibility nurses enjoyed there, even on nights as grueling as this one had been.

As she headed out the door, she lifted her arms, trying to stretch the tightness out of her muscles. One advantage of being so busy was that it had helped keep her mind off her inevitable meeting with Jase. She knew she was going to be made accountable for letting Becky ride Amber.

Just as she approached the elevator, she heard Debbie calling out and turned to see her jogging up the hallway, her emerald eyes aglow and her face wreathed in smiles.

"Whew! I'm glad I caught you. A great-looking guy is at the desk asking for you."

Now that she had heard Debbie's announcement, Reba wished she could hop into the elevator and be whisked away, for she had little doubt who the man was. In her bone-weary state she dreaded having to deal with Becky's father.

Reba kept the pace slow as they returned to the station. "It's probably Jase Kingsford. I told you about his daughter falling, remember?" Reba tried to recall all that she'd told Debbie the night before, when the emotional strain of Becky's accident had her going in circles. Reba had told a lot of half-truths to Debbie during the past two weeks, needing to explain her sudden purchase of a horse and her interest in a young girl named Becky. Every new complication made her story harder to keep straight.

Debbie scrutinized Reba. "He seemed very curious about you. Is there something going on between you two?"

"Going on?" Reba released an exasperated laugh. "I don't even know if I like him!" That part was true; she wasn't sure she approved of Jase. But she was terribly aware of him as a man. And that she didn't like at all.

As soon as Jase saw Reba approach, he left the desk to meet her. The instant their eyes met, she felt as if she were being swept into a raging tide. Her heart began to pound, and her knees seemed to lose their strength. *This is ridiculous!* she scolded herself. *Get hold of yourself, McCallister.* She braced her shoulders, collecting herself with an effort.

He smiled softly, and she was lost again. A telltale warmth spread from her neck upward.

Jase walked toward Reba, the sight of her making him feel as though the day had taken a sudden bright turn. Remarkable, since his mood that morning had started out as bleak as the dreary weather that had settled in on Lake Washington. He'd lain in bed, looking out the window at the cloudy sky blending almost without a line into the steel-gray water. Groggy and stiff, he'd waited for Becky to bring him coffee and the paper—comics on top to read together in bed—as was their normal Sunday routine. And then he'd remembered. Becky was in the hospital.

He'd dragged his tired body from the sheets and showered and dressed hurriedly so that he'd have some extra time to talk to Reba before Becky was released. He'd told himself that it was parental concern that caused him to want to see Reba. But now that he was here, he was glad in an unexpected way. Even in a uniform, Reba possessed the sweet allure that had enticed him at the show.

"Perfect timing. You're just starting your break. Let me buy you brunch in the cafeteria."

"All right," she said. "That sounds fine." But her dark eyes were guarded.

Heading for the bank of elevators, they walked side by side through the corridor busy with visitors and patients. The intercom's melodious call for doctors combined with the smells of disinfectant, badges and medicine to create a separate world. Jase noticed that beneath the controlled environment a feeling of tension pervaded, much like that at the newspaper where one could never be sure what would happen next, when all hell might break loose. He sensed the same pressure beneath Reba's composed exterior and wasn't pleased to be the cause of it.

The crowd in the elevator pushed them together, and they each whispered hasty apologies. Reba rubbed the tingling spot where his arm had briefly brushed against hers, overwhelmed by the disturbing effect he had on her. Until that moment she'd clung to the hope that the physical attraction between them had been fabricated in her overactive imagination. But now, here, with Jase standing so near and her pulse racing in response, she knew it was all too real.

When the elevator stopped, Reba stepped out first, wanting to distance herself from Jase. "Have you already been up to see Becky?" she asked as they entered the cafeteria. When he indicated he hadn't, she continued in a casual manner, "I saw her this morning. I'm happy to report she's alive and kicking and giving Dr. Estrada a terrible time with all her questions."

"That sounds like her." The mental picture of Becky tormenting their family doctor made Jase crack a smile. At the self-serve counter he stepped up behind Reba and took a tray. "She's being released this morning. I'm here to take her home."

"She doesn't even have a bruise," Reba remarked, thinking Jase would be pleased to hear that.

"Yes. She was damn lucky this time."

His suddenly icy tone seemed to warn of chilling conversation to come, and Reba geared up for it by taking a long draw of her black coffee as soon as she'd filled her cup. Jase's tray was empty except for his own coffee with cream, and Reba felt too uneasy to eat. She let him pay and find them a table.

"I'm on the brink of forbidding her to go to the stables anymore," he said without preamble as soon as they were seated.

She blinked at him, caught by surprise. "But Becky loves horses."

He glanced away, his expression unreadable. "Many young girls go through a horse-crazy phase."

"Oh, but her interest in them is more than that." Reba cupped her drink with rigid fingers as she groped for something to say that might change his mind. "Jase, I know I have no right to interfere, but I think keeping her from riding would be a cruel thing to do." As soon as the hasty words were out, she wished she could retract them. Fatigue had robbed her of her normal diplomacy.

His quick gaze, like a shard of sharp blue ice, impaled Reba. "I'm only worried about her safety. I can assure you I'd never be cruel to my daughter."

"Of course not," she replied at once, her tone conciliatory. "I'm not saying you would . . . on purpose." His features remained stony. She gave herself a mental kick for going about this in such a doltish way. She recalled her mother's attempts to teach her the fine art of tact, along with other mannerly rules such as remembering to send her elderly maiden aunt a thank-you note for the baby doll with stroller she'd sent Reba for her twelfth birthday. They'd shared a laugh over the inappropriate gift and made a grand presentation over giving the doll to the little neighbor girl. Her mother's gentle teaching had made life fun and easy. She desperately wanted Jase to make Becky's life fun and easy, too.

Reba started on a new tack. "I don't think Becky would understand."

"She understands I only want to protect her." He cocked his head and narrowed his eyes. "Didn't she tell you *why* I don't like her riding?"

"Yes. She told me, Jase." Becky had told her that her father didn't like horses and that he was determined to have her share her interest in other sports. Becky had called his attitude "irrational." Reba met Jase's fierce blue gaze. He certainly did seem irrational on the subject. Not knowing how else to reach him, she decided to reveal a little of her own history. She shifted forward for emphasis but strove to make her voice calm and reasonable. "I empathize with Becky because I was about her age when my own mother died," Reba explained. "She'd done all the raising of my brother and me, so when Dad had to take over, he didn't know what to do with us. He made the rules. My brother and I were expected to obey. No discussion allowed. It caused me to be very rebellious." She searched for a way to link her experience with Becky's in a manner that wouldn't further offend Jase. "What I'm trying to say is that Becky is willful," she continued carefully. "Just as I once was. She resents unnecessary restriction."

"I think I know best how to deal with my daughter," he returned, then softened his voice. "I'm not as unreasonable as you may think I am, Reba. Finding the balance between too lax and too firm is difficult sometimes. I suppose it's no different from learning to handle a spirited horse."

His words prompted her. "Oh, about Becky's riding Amber...I know I owe you an explanation and an apology. I was the one who suggested it. I intend to take the blame."

"Not all of it," Jase countered. "Becky shouldn't have ridden the mare. She knows I feel that horse is too highstrung for her."

"Amber is spirited, but no more so than the horses she rides during her lessons. Becky is such an excellent rider that I didn't see the harm in it. There wouldn't have been a problem if someone hadn't thrown a firecracker under Amber's belly. Any animal would have reacted that way."

"Perhaps."

She suppressed her irritation. "I would never have allowed Becky to ride Amber if I thought there was danger involved."

"Becky told me you didn't know much about horses," he pointed out. "That you hadn't ridden since you were a teenager." He took a long drink of coffee, studying her over the rim of the cup. "I believe you had good intentions—but poor judgment."

She felt heat rising to her face and struggled to keep from lashing out. Poor judgment, indeed!

"I'm not going to let Becky off the hook," Jase continued. "She knew she was doing wrong. She shouldn't have snuck out of the house to go to the show, and she shouldn't have ridden your horse."

"And for these crimes you'd keep her from her favorite activity forever?" Reba was flabbergasted at the injustice.

"There's good cause for my feelings. Frankly, that fall she took scared the life out of me."

"But that was a fluke accident. There's a risk factor in every sport. Besides, Becky's a natural athlete." She leaned sideways to scan Jase's athletic body, liking what she saw despite her raw temper. "Just as you appear to be. Haven't you ever scared the life out of anyone?"

Jase couldn't keep a quick smile from spreading across his face. He saw Reba's pretty features relax, and a wave of relief washed over him. The day before she had stirred feelings within him he'd forgotten he had, and he sensed she was interested in him, as well. The thought of their budding relationship ending over this dispute was intolerable.

"I've even scared the life out of myself a few times," he admitted.

"Aha!" Reba gave a knowing nod. "What's your specialty?"

"Boating and scuba diving in Puget Sound. A little snow skiing at Snoqualmie or Mount Baker. With all the water we have here and the Cascade Mountains an hour's drive from Seattle, who could help but take advantage of it?"

"Ah, yes. Scuba diving. Drownings. The bends." Her huge brown eyes sparked. "Now there's some injuries for you."

Jase fought to keep from laughing at his own ridiculous position in the debate. "You're not going to criticize snow skiing?" he asked with mock outrage.

"I don't have to. The walking wounded speak for themselves."

He smiled, his attention caught by the rose-petal curve of her lips. "You've got me there." He continued to gaze at her hungrily until her thick, dark lashes fluttered downward. She gave her watch a jerky glance.

"I have to be getting back." When she looked at him again, her eyes had clouded, as if she were closing him out.

He wasn't ready to part company. "I'll go down with you."

"That's not necessary." Reba rose, thinking how pleased her mother would have been with that remark when she had wanted to shout no and bolt for the door. It wasn't the argument over Becky's riding that made her so anxious to depart, but rather the attraction growing between them. She knew she must avoid any personal involvement with Jase. The danger was plainly evident.

"I insist on walking you back," he said, rising.

Jase stayed close to Reba's side and kept the atmosphere light by making small talk as they headed for the elevators. When the doors slid open, he followed her inside, the elevator empty this time. In the cloistered space her potent femininity wrapped around him, making his heart pound. He had a sudden urge to fold her into his arms—but then the elevator came to a halt, and the doors opened. He stepped out behind her and reached for her hand. "Wait," he commanded.

Trapped by the strong fingers surrounding her wrist, Reba felt a wave of sensuality wash through her, intensifying her need to escape.

"Let me take you for something to eat when you get off work today." His tone was low and intense. "I'd like to talk to you more about Becky."

He'd appealed to the one topic that weakened her, but her good sense won out. "I can't." She pulled her hand away slightly, and he let her go. "This is the fourth day in a row of long shifts for me, and I have to work again tonight. I'm just going to collapse when I get home—"

Her excuses were cut short by a woman's cries. "No! Let me out of here! I have to see her!"

The distraught voice emanated from the minor surgery room in the examining wing. Glad for any excuse to get away from Jase, Reba excused herself. She jogged past the nurses' station and down the hallway to the room at the end.

Larry Howes, the new intern, stood over the examining table holding a compress against a young woman's head while Debbie took her blood pressure.

The patient started to rise, and Larry put a heavy hand on her shoulder. "Hold it, young lady," he said. "You're not going anywhere right now."

"I have to get out of here," the young woman cried. "I need to see my baby. I know she's hurt!"

Reba's stomach contracted at the woman's frantic pleas. She slid a quick glance to Larry, asking him with her eyes if the child indeed was injured.

Larry struggled to keep the compress in place. "The baby's fine," he assured both the patient and Reba. "She was strapped into her car seat. She's safe and sound in the next room."

"We keep telling her that, but she's pretty upset," Debbie said.

"Let me see my baby!" Tears streamed down the young woman's cheeks. "If she's not hurt, why can't I see her?"

Her hysteria worked at Reba's composure. Unaccountably she felt the young woman's fear as though it were her own child in the other room.

Larry hung on to the compress as he attempted to keep the distraught mother on the table. "Your baby wasn't hurt at all. Your only problem is this scalp laceration. We have to get it sutured."

Reba placed a kind hand on the patient's shoulder. "I know you want to see your baby. We're going to get your baby." She spoke in a slow repetitive tone as she looked into the young woman's glazed eyes. "Just as soon as you calm down, we're going to get your baby."

Her sobs lessened.

"You must be a calm mother so that you don't scare your baby. Now do what I say to get under control. Take a deep breath." Reba demonstrated, hoping it would help her hang on to her own restraint. It was unlike her to be so affected by a patient. She had always prided herself on being a professional, but this situation struck an emotional chord within her.

The young woman's chest shuddered.

"Nice and slow," Reba repeated. "That's right. Now another one. You're calming down now. You're doing fine. We're going to get your cut under control, too. So we can get your baby."

The patient nodded, her gaze moving from Reba's face to fix on something behind her. Reba looked back over her shoulder, her eyes suddenly meeting Jase's. She masked her expression, not wanting any trace of emotion to be detected by him.

She motioned toward the door with her head. "You'll have to leave," she ordered.

He held her gaze for a long moment before he obeyed. Relieved, Reba turned back to the patient and checked the laceration with Larry.

"The suturing can wait a few minutes," he said.

Jase was nowhere to be seen as she went to fetch the baby sleeping in the bassinet in the next examining room. Her fingers trembled when she held the warm pink bundle against her chest. Bending her head, Reba brushed her cheek against the blond hair plastered against the infant's forehead. She smelled of that wonderful clean baby smell, her breath milky. A resurgence of something long repressed swelled in Reba's heart, an ache painful and sweet. She carried the child to her waiting mother and whispered, "She's asleep." She helped the young woman hold her baby.

The mother looked up at Reba. "Thank you," she murmured, and Reba knew she must be wondering why there were tears in a nurse's eyes.

After a few minutes Reba said, "I'll take her back now, before she wakes." She carried the infant back to the bassinet. After tucking her in, Reba turned away from the baby with a wrench that tore at her insides. A terrible sense of loss, loss of her own child, swept over her. The emotion drained her. She could not remember when she'd last felt so physically and mentally exhausted.

Knowing Larry and Debbie could handle things now without her, she resolutely set one foot in front of the other and headed for the nurses' station. She struggled to pull herself together. This kind of extreme personal reaction to a hospital emergency was unlike her, and she had no patience with it.

But she felt so tired. Finally she leaned a shoulder against the cool plaster wall to rest for a moment. A hand touched the small of her back, causing her to draw in a startled breath.

"You're exhausted," came Jase's familiar deep voice. Not giving her time to say a word, he circled her waist in a powerful embrace that could have held all her weight if needed. Taking complete command, he led her into a dark, empty side room.

Surprised by Jase's forcefulness, Reba found herself alone with him before she'd had time to gather her wits. She shook her head, trying to clear her mind. "What are you doing?" she demanded. Her protest ended in a gasp when he tightened his hold on her, drawing her against him so that her breasts pressed against his chest.

"I'm taking you from the battleground for a minute," he said. "You looked as though you were about to faint out there in the hallway. You're going to take time out until you get control of yourself."

But his gruff concern only made her feel weaker. When he eased her head to his shoulder, she suddenly began to cry, moisture rolling in a hot torrent down her cheeks. He held her close and stroked her hair in an effort to calm her. After what seemed an eternity, he produced a handkerchief and blotted the wetness away with efficient pats.

"I feel so ridiculous," she choked out with the last of her tears. She couldn't believe she was actually weeping in Jase Kingsford's arms. She must have lost her mind. Placing her shaky hands on his chest, she made an effort to create a barrier between them. "I'm fine now."

"I don't think you're fine at all. And I don't intend to let you go just yet."

She wanted to resist him, but his determination was too much for her. Surrendering, she let her body lean heavily against his. Despite her inner turmoil, she cherished the comfort and protection of his embrace. When he moved his hand back to look at her, she thought he might kiss her, and a delicious yearning for it spiraled through her. But he only drew in a deep breath and glanced away.

She let her eyelids close drowsily and her head rest on his shoulder again. In the quiet darkness she forgot the outside world, the page of the intercom speaker in the hallway outside only the faintest reminder. For an irrational moment she allowed herself to linger in his embrace. Her heart throbbed and his responded, pounding against her breasts. She moved her hands down his broad chest and around his lean waist, pressing her fingers into her sweater to feel the ridges of muscles along his spine. He stiffened and lowered his hands to her waist. Reba felt his forceful grip burning through the fabric of her dress, and as he arched her against him, she drew in a sharp breath.

The sensual contact brought her back to her senses. Amazed at herself for allowing things to get so out of hand, Reba drew herself up, straightening her spine and tensing her muscles. The subtle change was detected by

Jase, who removed his hands from their intimate position.

She stepped back, looking down at her uniform, which she smoothed with short, rapid strokes. "You must think I'm a complete idiot." Giving an abrupt, self-conscious laugh, she rushed on. "I don't normally succumb to crying fits."

"I watched you with that patient. You're under tremendous stress on this job."

"Yes," Reba agreed, snatching up the ideal excuse. "It's been a long, hard night."

There was a moment of contemplative silence before Jase said, "Something tells me it's more than that."

It was a great deal more than that. Painful emotions, long submerged in her past, had boiled to the surface and spilled over. But she could never tell Jase that.

"It's burnout, that's all. You just witnessed how stressful the ER can be. We never know what kind of problem is coming next."

"Are you sure you're okay?"

"Quite." She turned toward the door.

He reached out to grasp her wrist. At his touch Reba felt her flesh weaken, and she almost allowed herself to move back into his arms.

"Reba. I want to see you again. Next weekend." It wasn't so much a request as it was a velvet-toned command.

How she longed to say yes, yes, she would. Her better judgment prevailed by the slimmest margin. "It's not possible. I don't have a weekend off until the end of October."

"Okay. When is your first day off?"

"Thursday," she murmured.

"It's a date, then?" When she hesitated, his thumb caressed the skin on the back of her hand, causing shivers to run up her arm. "Since you seem to want to be Becky's friend, I have a parental right to get to know you."

She realized he had a point. And she did want to learn more about him and his relationship with Becky. She would just have to restrain her emotions. "I *would* like to talk to you before you make any decisions about Becky's riding. Before you do something rash."

"I'm never rash," he said.

But Jase knew that at least in Reba's case it wasn't true. Having her in his arms had sparked the rashest feelings he'd ever known.

3

"NO, NO, NO! Don't even think about it," Reba warned Bushka, who gazed up at her with soulful eyes and drooping tongue.

Making a wide detour around the great yellow bush of a dog, Reba entered the kitchen to pour a cup of coffee. She had enough on her mind without having Bushka jump up and soil her outfit. She'd put a great deal of thought into choosing the pastel-pink sweater dress, hoping to present a sophisticated—but not provocative—image. Sparks had already flared between her and Jase; encouraging flames was the last thing she wanted to do.

And resisting him would prove hard enough as it was. He had been on her mind all week.

Her fear that her emotions would take control had almost caused her to make excuses when Jase had phoned the day before. He evidently possessed the instincts of a strategist; when he'd heard the hesitation in her voice, he'd reminded her that he wanted her advice on handling Becky. Her daughter's happiness meant everything to Reba. She must find a way to smooth Becky and Jase's relationship, to convince him to be more sympathetic toward Becky's feelings about horses. If that called for seeing more of Jase than she felt comfortable with, so be it.

The old oak school clock on the kitchen wall told her she had twenty minutes before Jase was due to pick her up, and her nerves were already acting up. To keep her mind off Jase while she waited for him to arrive, Reba decided to add the newspaper photo of Becky to the others in her meager collection. Taking her coffee with her, she went into the living room and pulled a photo album from the bottom drawer of her desk.

She sat on the couch, placed the album on her lap and slowly opened it. Though the pictures had been taken twelve years before, the searing pain of loss she'd suffered then had not diminished, and no doubt never would.

Reba remembered the moment the nurse had carried Becky into her hospital room for the first time and said, "Here's your baby." Even then, underlying the normal emotions of giddiness, relief and ecstasy lurked fear for her little daughter's future.

Except for Birdie, the nurse who ran the maternity shelter where Reba stayed, no one visited her in the hospital. She hadn't seen her boyfriend, Steven, for months. Her father had refused to even acknowledge Becky, let alone allow Reba to return home with her. Keeping Becky meant striking out alone into the world—a feat that at barely sixteen she was entirely unprepared for. Nevertheless, she would have tried to make a go of it if Steven had been at her side.

Eighteen-year-old Steven had seemed so much more mature than the other boys she'd known, but when she'd told him she'd accidentally become pregnant, his reaction had disappointed her. Then, when he'd disappeared, she'd hated him. She didn't hate him anymore. Though sometimes she wondered what had become of him, she rarely thought of him at all.

Becky hadn't mentioned the fact that she was adopted, but Reba felt certain she knew. Reba wondered if Becky and Jase believed Becky had been deserted by an uncaring mother. If only she could explain, Reba thought in frustration, that if she'd kept Becky, her father would not have allowed her to return home. She would have had to drop out of school, and would no doubt have ended up on welfare. She wished she could tell Jase and Becky the whole story and make them understand that adoption was the only chance Becky had for a better life. If only they could feel the pain that decision had cost her.

Reba turned the pages of the album until she came to a photograph of Birdie. Birdie's wise counsel had helped her accept the situation and chart a course for the future, but after Reba left Birdie's home, she had never gone back to visit. Even though she loved Birdie and would always be grateful to her, that part of her life just hurt too much. Birdie wasn't the only one she'd shut out; she saw her father rarely.

She closed the album and started to put it away, then decided to leave it out to look at again later. Now that she'd found Becky, the memories didn't tear at her heart with such force.

She heard the sound of a car turning into the driveway, and her pulse leaped. Jase. Feeling much more eager than she had a right to feel, Reba snatched up her coat to meet him outside. When she closed the front door behind her, he was already out of a silver BMW. That he had a town car, as well as the Bronco, didn't surprise her. In fact, she had expected Jase to be more formally dressed, in keeping with his life-style as a prominent businessman. Instead, he looked casual and as disturbingly handsome as she remembered in slim-fitting jeans and a black windbreaker.

"I think I'm overdressed." Reba hovered on the stoop, gripping the cold wrought-iron railing. "Should I change?"

"No. Don't. You look wonderful." Jase opened the passenger door for her, thinking she was an exquisite sight in her soft pink dress, with her cocoa-brown hair bouncing in tight curls to her shoulders. "You look like you're wrapped in pink cotton candy."

"It looks like rain," she said, the excitement churning in her veins making her feel as giddy as an adolescent. "I hope I don't melt."

After settling her into the passenger seat, Jase went around to the driver's side, taking his time in order to purge from his mind the image of Reba with her dress washed away. He concentrated instead on her home, wondering why a single woman would choose a house over an apartment. The place was clean and neat but nothing fancy, just a small white box with a door smack in the center and a window on either side. As he slid inside the car, he said, "I'm surprised you have a house instead of an apartment near the hospital. Isn't it inconvenient? Especially with the hours you seem to work."

"To tell you the truth, I wasn't too sure about renting a house. But Max insisted."

Jase's hand stalled on the ignition key. He clamped down on the turmoil raging inside him at the distinct possibility that this bright and sexy woman had already been claimed. This was his first date since

Carolyn's death, and he didn't know if he was up to invading another man's territory. He decided it would be wise to clear up a few matters at the outset. "Reba, I never asked you about your private life. I know you're not married—"

"And just how do you know that?"

"I queried the redhead at the hospital desk," he admitted. "It's the journalist in me, I guess, always asking questions about something—or someone—I'm interested in. I'm sorry that it upsets you."

She would have to have a talk with Debbie, Reba decided. Though Debbie undoubtedly meant well, giving out personal information to virtual strangers— no matter how attractive—was dangerous. "I don't have a 'significant other' or whatever the phrase is these days. Max is my cat. I adopted him from a little girl who was standing in front of the grocery store with a whole box of kitties to give away. Max looked up at me with these huge eyes that asked, 'Are you my new mommy?' What could I do?"

Jase started the engine, the stiffness gone from his shoulders. "And the cat asked you to rent this house."

"Not in words, but he had other ways to communicate." Just then a sleek black feline leaped from between the rhododendron bushes to land on the hood of Reba's old Volkswagen parked in the sloping drive. "That's him," she said. "You see, some cats are the outdoors type. They go crazy if they're cooped up inside all the time. Max shredded the curtains, used the planter as a litter box and tried to escape every time I opened the door. It came down to either giving up him or the apartment."

Jase backed onto the street and started down the hill she lived on. "And you didn't choose the easier of the two. Interesting. You're a gal with a mind of her own. Your good traits are definitely outweighing the bad." He paused to glance in her direction and grin. "Come to think of it, there are no bad. You're perfect."

If this was meant to flatter her, it worked, as Reba felt a tingly pleasure suffusing her from the ends of her toes to the tips of her ears. She suddenly forgave Debbie her indiscretion. Jase Kingsford, when charming, was irresistible.

"I just refused this time to let difficult circumstances control my happiness," Reba explained. She knew the extra expense of renting a house must seem foolish to him, despite his outward approval. "I was being selfish—not a good trait at all. I simply wanted very much to keep my cat."

Reba turned her face toward her window, pretending to watch the world roll by, and worried that she'd revealed too much. It didn't take a degree in psychology to figure out that her pets took the place of children in her life. Even though she'd wanted Becky to go to a better home than she could provide, regrets had always plagued her. She watched the sun break through the clouds, the rays beaming into the car to shower them with sudden brightness. That was all in the past, she reminded herself. The future seemed as bright as the sunlight. She'd found Becky again. And here she was with Jase Kingsford, who was making it so easy for her to be a long-lasting fixture in her daughter's life.

Jase drove them out of Reba's neighborhood of small homes and into a heavy stream of traffic. Now, instead of houses, clusters of condominiums flanked the road.

"It's hard to believe I rode my bike past cornfields on this stretch when I was a kid."

She slanted a glance at him, considering his narrow blond mustache, his well-developed mature physique. Even though she guessed him to be about forty, it wasn't hard to imagine him as a boy. Although Jase's family was affluent, she pictured him as an ambitious youngster, no doubt starting to work as a paper carrier. Of course he'd played ball in Little League, too. And gone fishing with his dad . . . and eaten apple pie his mother had baked. The all-American boy who'd grown into Mr. Upstanding Citizen. She'd never thought she'd like the type, yet here she was falling more and more under his spell.

To divert the train of her thoughts, she returned to the neutral topic. "I'm sure you never guessed there would be high rises on this side of Lake Washington."

"I didn't mean to give you the idea it was all farmers living here when I was a kid. There was a good-sized contingent of city folks like my parents, who chose to live on the east side. Actually the neighborhood Becky and I live in hasn't changed character too much. Have you ever been to Hunt's Point?"

Reba's fingers jerked in nervous reaction. "Maybe once on a Sunday drive. I don't recall."

"It's a very homey area. At least it has great sentiment for me. I decided to move into the old place when my parents retired to Palm Springs last winter. I suppose I was seeking roots for Becky and me. I had a happy childhood there and I wanted the same for Becky."

"That's nice, Jase," Reba said, incredibly pleased with him.

He covered up his embarrassment at her praise with an exaggerated shrug. "What could I do? We lived in a seventh-floor condo before, and she was shredding the curtains and—"

"Jase." Reba laughed out his name. "It's okay for men to show their emotions. It's considered very manly these days."

He glanced over, heating her face with the smoldering interest in his eyes. "With you that's no problem at all. I think I've been very clear about what I feel for you."

Reba felt as though her cheeks had caught fire. Her burgeoning feelings for him had shown. She had led him on. And it was wrong, wrong, wrong. Now what was she going to do? Her head swam in confusion.

She could think of nothing more to say. Jase's intimate words had wiped her brain clean of rational thought. The conversation lapsed as they began passing affluent neighborhoods of modern homes, one architect's dream after another. She gazed distractedly at the young planted trees, their autumn yellow leaves contrasting with the dark green needles of native firs. Those tall evergreen trees, nearly as numerous in the suburbs as in the countryside, were what made the Pacific Northwest cities unique and dear to Reba. She couldn't imagine living far from the trees and mountains and water. But it wasn't the landscape that made this area special to her now, she realized. It was because Becky and Jase lived here. Without them she somehow knew that her beloved Seattle would feel like a dismal place, indeed.

Lost in her thoughts, Reba was surprised when he took a turn and headed toward the roadway marked by the silvery driftwood sign, Hunt's Point.

"Where are we going?" she asked, growing uncomfortable.

"To lunch as promised."

She looked at him sideways. "At your home?"

"No, at my favorite restaurant, via the home port." He grinned. "Do you know that according to some experts, a woman doesn't begin to fall in love with a man until he's fed her? I don't know whether I agree, but with you, special lady, I'm not taking any chances."

By the time he'd finished the outrageous speech, they'd turned through the open wrought-iron gates and were headed down a winding drive toward a three-story white clapboard house. Not able to deal with her raging emotions, she concentrated on surveying Jase's home.

"How do you like the place?" he asked her.

"It's impressive," she murmured. But what caught her eye was that the house was so much more than grand. It possessed a homey, lived-in look with a soccer ball in the yard, a wreath of dried flowers on the front door and potted plants in the windows. Beyond the house spread vast Lake Washington, its surface sprinkled with glitter in the sunlight. Jase pulled up to a three-car garage almost hidden by massive laurel hedges and birch trees.

"Jase," Reba said, readying herself for a speech as he helped her from the car. Her back was to the door, and he didn't move aside but stood there blocking her passage. Despite her disadvantaged position, she decided to make a stance there instead of scooting off to the side.

"Jase," she repeated more firmly. "We need to get something straight before we go on. I've got the impression you're looking for a more, ah, intense relationship than I am. I think that we should stick to building a friendship."

He leaned closer, unnerving her with his intense gaze on her mouth. "I agree. One hundred percent."

"Oh. Well, that's good." Relief mingled with despair.

"First friends." His eyes held hers, and a silent knowledge that they were undeniably drawn to each other flowed between them. "Then friendly lovers."

"No!" She dragged her gaze from the lethal potency of his. "You didn't listen—" His palm cupped her chin, silencing her.

"Stop thinking, Reba. Just feel," he murmured, not giving her time to protest before he brushed his lips over hers ever so lightly, as if he was testing her response. Her muscles, her willpower seemed to dissolve at his touch, and when his brief kiss ended, she was aghast to discover how eager she was for more of the same. His blue eyes smiled down at her, speaking his awareness of the disturbing effect he had on her. He moved closer, letting his hands fall to the small of her back and molding her body to his. It was at that moment she should have pleaded for him to stop, but the words had dammed in her throat.

As she knew he would, he took her silence as a sign of consent. He moved his mouth down to hers, suddenly no longer gentle. He was kissing her as she'd never before been kissed—or maybe it was that she'd never before responded with such instant desire. She gripped his firm waist with her fingers, and then she had her arms around him, pulling him closer. Her bones felt liquid and her loins alive with fire. Though she had acknowledged that she found him attractive, she was only now discovering fully the powerful sensual effect he had on her. She realized their relationship was on the brink of something . . . something that both thrilled and terrified her.

Jase released her mouth and drew in a ragged breath. "That kiss is what I've been waiting for ever since we met." He held her close, talking into her hair. "I want you to know I won't rush you into anything you're not ready for—but I believe in total honesty in life. I'm telling you now that I have no intention of putting limitations on our relationship." They parted enough so that his eyes, dusky with desire, could look deeply into hers. "Now, do you still want to have lunch with me?"

She knew she should say no. She knew it, and yet the warnings in her mind seemed unreal. The only real thing on earth at that moment was the man standing so close to her. His gaze had the effect of a brisk autumn wind, blowing her doubts and fears away. This head-reeling, heart-pounding sensation she felt couldn't be wrong.

"Just point me in the direction of the food," she said, still breathless from his kiss, her eyes glowing with wonderment.

He caressed her mouth with his one last time. "Come on," he said, his chiseled lips curving in a pleased smile. "I'll give you the ten-cent tour of the grounds before we head out."

Reba, though still puzzled as to why he'd brought her to his home, was willing to follow his lead. At that moment, as dizzy-minded as she felt, she would have followed him anywhere.

He reached for her hand and guided her to one side of the house where an Olympic-sized pool sparkled like an aquamarine in the crown of landscaped terraces that rounded down to the lake. She gazed around, trying to take it all in. At a leisurely pace Jase led her to the back of the house where a large inviting porch offered a breathtaking view. The sky remained scattered with clouds, a familiar sight since Seattle averaged more than two hundred gray days per year. As a cloud covered the sun, the huge lake turned to pewter. Beyond the water, beyond the cityscape, the Olympic mountains rose like a line of white steeples.

"On the other side of the house is the tennis court, but let's cut the tour short and go down to the dock." He glanced up at the ever-changing sky. "This weather does look unpredictable. Being out on the lake in the rain is not my idea of fun."

Reba blinked up at him. "We're going out on a boat?"

"Any objections? You like boats, don't you?"

Reba shrugged, bemused by it all. "I've never been on one before." She laughed at his stunned expression. "I know! It's ridiculous, isn't it? Especially when Seattle has more boats per capita than any other city in the country."

"Let's not waste any precious time." If anything, Reba decided her admission brought a gleam of new interest to his expression.

Once out on the lake, any doubts she may have had about boating disappeared. When Jase opened the throttle to send the big blue-and-white cabin cruiser roaring across the lake, she felt as though they were flying.

"Oh, Jase! I love it!" she cried out, laughing like a thrilled child. "Thank you. I'll never forget this."

After a while Jase cut back the engines. He looked over at her seated in the swivel chair next to his, and Reba noticed a special intensity glowing in his eyes as they swept her excitement-flushed face.

"You're so refreshing," he said, his voice loud enough to be heard, but oddly intimate at the same time. "My wife didn't care for boating. Besides, her family keeps a yacht in the Bahamas, so the *Rebecca Marie* was a big step down in the thrill department."

"Do you miss her very much still?" Uneasiness rose within her at the thought.

"I think about her often, but I don't pine for her in the way you mean. She was a fine woman in many ways and a very good mother to Becky."

Reba was relieved, not only because he wasn't carrying a torch for his wife, but also because she had wondered about Becky's relationship with her adopted mother.

"Have you ever been married, Reba?"

"No," she answered before looking teasingly at him. "You mean you didn't get that information from Debbie, too?"

"Only the vital statistics: twenty-eight, single, size seven shoe."

Reba laughed. "That's a size seven dress, too, in case you're planning to restock my closet."

"Mmm, that's a thought. I'd dress you in silk and satin, so you'd always be soft to the touch."

The type of silk and satin garments that immediately came to Reba's mind were the intimate variety, sexy things that a man would give only to his lover. "I'd like to see the patients' expressions if I came to work in a red satin nurse's uniform instead of our standard white cotton. I'd make quite an impression."

"I think you make quite an impression just the way you are," he said as he adjusted the chrome controls and then vacated his captain's seat to come stand behind her. "I also think it's time for you to learn how to handle a boat. Go ahead and steer."

She hesitated. "I've never done this before."

"Try it. You have that sensitive touch that sensitive boats like this one love."

"I can't believe you would trust an amateur like me with this beautiful boat."

"I have complete confidence in you." He grinned. "Besides, what could happen?"

"Right," she returned, deadpan. "Okay, Captain Courageous, here goes nothing." She gripped the wheel, unable to truly concentrate with Jase's body pressing against her back.

He leaned down, brushing his chest against her shoulders as he pointed out the compass dial in the panel of controls. "Keep the needle pointing west," he directed. "Now this is how you increase your speed." Before Reba could say she didn't want to go faster, he took her hand and placed it on the cool metal throttle. His warm, strong fingers tightened on hers, and he pushed her hand forward. One of the engines roared, and she laughed excitedly. "Feel that?" he asked, bending close as the cruiser flew over the waves. She couldn't distinguish between the throb of the motors and the throb of her own blood when he was so near.

"Yes. I definitely feel something," she murmured.

"Are you in control?"

She'd never felt so out of control in her life. "I think I can handle it until we get to Cape Horn. Then you'd better take over."

She heard his chuckle against her ear before he planted a kiss on her neck. He removed his fingers from hers and stepped back. Her hand felt deserted, and her back missed his body heat. She tried to keep her mind focused on the University of Washington Husky Stadium, which drew nearer as they sped across the lake.

"Better slow down now," he advised. "There's narrowing traffic ahead." The Gothic campus of the university bordered their route by canal to Lake Union. Along the shores of the campus, pleasure boats shared mooring with houseboats, some old with weatherbeaten paint, others strikingly modern in the natural grays and browns Northwesterners seemed to prefer. The lake ahead was alive with crafts of every description. "It's getting pretty crowded," Jase commented, stepping close behind her again.

Water-loving Seattleites, taking advantage of any bit of sunshine, were out in droves. A slim speedboat crossed in front of them, its spray dancing against the backdrop of city skyscrapers. A moment later their cabin cruiser bounced over the wake. "Do you want to take over?" she asked, feeling as she had when, as a student driver, she'd first taken a car across a narrow bridge in heavy traffic.

"That's all right. You're doing fine," Jase encouraged her, his nearness giving her confidence. "You're the original Miss Cool, Calm and Collected."

"You wouldn't say that if you knew how badly my knees were shaking," she confessed, laughing back at him. *Or how rapidly my heart is beating,* she added silently. She was constantly aware of his proximity. He directed her through Lake Union, which lay in the heart of Seattle and was busy with pleasure and commercial vessels. Even floatplanes used the lake as an airstrip.

At last he announced, "There's the Lakeside Restaurant dock ahead." A sailboat was pulling out. "We'll wait here till they're clear. Remember, sailboats always have the right of way."

"Aye, aye, Captain."

He covered her hand on the throttle with his again and brought the engine down to a gentle idle. The cruiser sloshed rhythmically at wait. The low vibrations of the engines seemed to penetrate Reba's flesh, permeating to her very core. As they waited for the sailboat to pass, Jase remained pressed close, causing the sexual tension in her body to steadily increase.

"All right, they're well cleared," Jase said. "Let's head in."

In her inexperience Reba pushed the throttle too eagerly, causing them to surge ahead.

That was when she saw it coming.

A small powerboat raced toward them, water cascading from either side of its bow. The open deck was crammed with young people, partying with beers in hand. The man at the wheel had his arms around a woman, and he faced away as though he was talking to someone instead of watching where he was going.

Panic surged up to grip Reba's throat, strangling her outcry. She stomped at the floor, instinctively trying to hit brakes that didn't exist in a boat.

"Jase!" she shouted, abandoning the controls. "Oh, my God, we're going to be killed!"

4

"DAMN IDIOTS!" Jase wheeled the cruiser hard to the left and avoided a collision by mere inches. By the time Reba recovered her heart from her throat, a police boat had brought the thoughtless revelers to a halt. From the pallor on Jase's face, he'd been just as frightened as she. Letting the cruiser idle, he reached for Reba and pulled her into the reassuring circle of his arms. "Thank God you weren't hurt," he muttered, his voice husky with restrained fury.

"Are you all right?" she asked shakily.

"I'm fine," he muttered, unconcerned about himself.

"Do you think people have nine lives like cats?" Though no longer scared, she was in no hurry to depart from the comfort of his embrace. "If so, I do think we just used one up."

"This year I've already lived through a diving mishap in Puget Sound and come close to being buried in an avalanche while helicopter skiing. I'd better be more careful. I might not survive until our next date."

"Oh, Jase. That's terrible. Does Becky know about those accidents?"

"Of course not. It would only worry her."

Aware of the advantage befallen her, Reba intended to make the most of it. "Well, you're not going to continue participating in those risky sports, are you?" She composed her features into an expression of utter seriousness. "Surely you've learned your lesson."

Jase released her, turning his outward attention to steering the boat toward the dock while he considered his reply. "Risky or not, those physical activities help relieve the stress of my work. I wouldn't find the same satisfaction in a game of croquet or a stroll in the park."

At that point Reba had to force away the sly smile that threatened to play across her face. She decided to hold her return volley until they were in the restaurant, and for the next few minutes their conversation was limited to the mechanics of getting the boat securely berthed. But once they'd been shown to a corner table, complete with an unobstructed view of the lake, she hesitated to bring up an uncomfortable subject. The day was so special that she hated to spoil it with an argument.

She relaxed in her chair, looking about with less interest in the nautical decor than in the man seated across from her. She was glad they'd arrived at the tail end of the lunch crowd, for the restaurant had a pleasant feeling of winding down about it.

After Jase had placed their orders of broiled salmon, a Seattle specialty, the waitress returned with a bottle of Riesling. As Jase poured, he asked Reba why she had chosen nursing as a career.

"That's a hard question," she said, trying to ignore the distracting touch of Jase's fingers on hers as he handed her a glass of the chilled wine. She placed a finger on her lips in thought. "From a practical aspect I suppose it was because nursing offered steady employment." Reba glanced at Jase. He looked intrigued with the subject . . . or was it her mouth he found so interesting? She couldn't tell but reveled in the attention nevertheless. "But that's not what made me choose that profession," she continued. "The truth is I have a nurturing nature. I love to take care of people, to help them when they're in need."

"I admire you. I've always believed nurses lack the wages and the respect they deserve."

Reba grinned and reached across the table to tap her glass against his. "I'll drink to that."

But Jase's curiosity about her work brought back memories of her past, and her smiles faded as she recalled the hardship of those times. After she'd signed the adoption papers, she had gone back to live with her father until the end of high school, when she had left home. She'd refused his offers to help her, instead taking a job as an aide in a hospital school for severely handicapped children and working her way through college. Jase would never know how many nights during those years she'd cried herself to sleep from sheer exhaustion, how many times she'd wanted to quit. But somehow she'd managed to graduate, and she'd realized then that she'd been driven to succeed by a desperate need to prove herself. She'd fought to retrieve her pride, lost at sixteen.

"Now that I've answered your question, it's my turn." Reba sat forward in the comfortable chair, propping her forearms on the table. "Did you always expect to run the newspaper?"

"I suppose I did," Jase said. "You see, my father was of the old school where children did as they were told and were expected to follow parental footsteps. I have a younger brother, Daniel, but from as early as I can remember, I was the one groomed to take over the *Examiner*."

"You don't sound as if you appreciated that very much," Reba remarked, already fascinated by his story.

He nodded. "I didn't mean to sound as though my father was a tyrant—or that I had no spine. I wouldn't have gone into the business if I hadn't enjoyed it. And Dad tried to see that I did. When I was ten, I began drawing a salary, writing for a column he invented just for me. It was called 'Kid's Korner' and ran every Saturday. Later I moved up to one called 'The Truth of the Matter,' where I exposed political lies and that sort of thing. Exciting stuff for a kid still in college. That was the column that hooked me on becoming a newspaperman. The thrill of digging for the truth and making it known was indescribable."

Reba glanced downward, not able to look into his discerning eyes. His passionate feelings about truthfulness reminded her that, no matter how their relationship developed, Jase would never forgive her for hiding her identity. Reba toyed with her wineglass, continuing to avoid his gaze until she could rein in her dismal thoughts. "What about your brother?" she asked, picking a safe topic. "Does he work for the paper, too?"

Jase leaned back into a comfortable position, placed his arms across his firm stomach and entwined his fingers. "No. I think my articles about politics intrigued him, though. Daniel decided to offer America at least one honest politician. Himself. He lives in Washington, D.C., now."

"So that makes you the only journalist in this generation of Kingsfords."

He quirked his mouth into a half smile. "I was evidently the one to inherit the news-hound genes."

She laughed. "Don't tell me you believe those tendencies are inherited?"

"Certainly. Didn't they teach you that in genetics?" He chuckled, his eyes glimmering with the good humor of someone having a wonderful time. "Here. Let me show you." He leaned forward and pushed up his sleeve to reveal his exposed underarm. "See for yourself. Ink runs in these veins."

The veins of his arm were prominent, the muscle and sinew well defined. Reba believed his arm was the most sensually masculine one she had ever seen. Reaching across the table, she traced the blue vein all the way down to his wrist. His pulse beat there light and quick, while her own seemed to resound through her whole body.

The return of the waitress with their meals put an abrupt end to the charged moment. They began to eat, and for a few minutes contented silence reigned. That no awkwardness accompanied the lull showed how far they'd progressed in their relationship, Reba thought as she enjoyed the food. She liked Jase's directness. His honest nature seemed revealed in all aspects of his life.

"Well, we do have something in common." Reba picked up the thread of conversation as she took a break from eating. "Our fathers both were the undisputed head of the household."

"Your father was like mine, then?"

"Mm-hmm. In quite a few ways. Like your father, he has many facets. He was a good provider, and he loved my mom and brother and me. And I remember a lot of fun times we had together, doing things like camping in the Cascades. But he was strong willed and stubborn, too. He's a longshoreman, so there was no family business for my brother and me to go into, but Dad had done his stint in the Navy, and he managed to convince my younger brother, Tom, to enlist. As for me, had simple expectations: finish high school, then work until a nice man with a steady job came along." Her expression grew pensive as she again recalled her teenage years. That Jase had discussed his own childhood paved the way for her to do the same. "After mother died, he was terrified that something would happen to me and became very overprotective. I guess what bothered me most was the unfairness of it. You see, while he enjoyed numerous activities with his buddies, I was expected to stay at home and clean house and study hard like a good girl. I wasn't even allowed to go out on dates. And there was no use arguing with him once he'd made up his mind. I never could talk to him. To cut this long story short—" she paused "—and also lend some significance to a certain current situation . . . I began lying and sneaking out of the house."

"You lied to your father," he said with distaste. "You don't seem the type, Reba."

She felt the fine hair on the back of her neck bristle. "I find it hard to believe a man so concerned with facing life honestly can be so single-minded. Can't you see the unfairness? And how overprotectiveness will cause rebellion?"

His eyes hardened. "No, I don't. I believe people should have the courage to stand up and fight for their rights—"

"Like a *man*?" Reba finished. "Perhaps a grown man should behave in that manner, but it makes a sneak out of a child. You can't expect mature behavior from a child who's up against an overprotective, autocratic adult."

A taut moment passed as they eyed each other warily. It was Jase who broke the silence.

"I have the distinct feeling that the point of this entire conversation has been to lecture me on parenthood," he said in a crisp, cool tone.

Reba shoved her half-finished meal aside. "Very observant of you."

Jase sat erect. "If you can restrain your emotions, maybe we can discuss this like two rational people." He crossed his arms. His entire body seemed to flex and harden, as though he was preparing to fight a long hard battle. "Now tell me what you're getting at."

Noticing the couple at the next table eyeing them, Reba took a calming breath. "Jase, forgive me that stupid outburst. I just got carried away. You see, I've never forgiven my father for his lack of understanding. We could never talk things out. It caused an unbridgeable rift in our relationship. I can't bear the thought of that happening to you and Becky."

Jase also inhaled a deep breath. He recalled breakfast with Becky that morning. It was true she hadn't seemed quite her normal, cheerful self, but that was to be expected since she was still on restriction. When he'd teasingly flipped a spoonful of marmalade onto her eggs, she'd laughed easily enough. They'd had a heart-to-heart discussion about his beginning to date again, and he'd asked her how she felt about his taking Reba to lunch. Since he had always stressed complete honesty in their relationship, he wanted to know her feelings. To his delight she was pleased. She even encouraged it. That wasn't the reaction of a distraught teenager.

He studied Reba for a minute, his expression thoughtful, before saying, "I'm honored you care so much. However, I do think you're making too much of this. Becky and I are very close . . . even if we have our disagreements at times."

"Will you still be close if you forbid her to go riding—you, the father who won't give up his own risky sports?" *There*, she thought, *let him try to get around that*.

"I don't think that's quite the same thing at all. And I think Becky understands that. If I make a firm ruling, she'll soon forget all about this horse business."

"I disagree. Becky's an intelligent, spirited girl who won't take senseless rules or heavy-handed discipline." Reba paused to add weight to her words. "You'd better give careful consideration to any decisions made about Becky's riding. You're underestimating the passion she has for the sport. She loves horses. She yearns for one of her own. She's not going to just forget about it."

"Once I get her away from the stable, her interests will turn to something else. I think it's just a matter of encouraging her to enjoy movies, or shopping."

"Becky is not like that. She won't just forget about horses." Reba's voice rose higher and higher in her agitation. "She's a deep, feeling person, Jase."

"I'm sure she'll feel just as deeply about which outfit to buy for school."

His patronizing smile caused exasperation to boil up within her. She whipped her linen napkin from her lap and slapped it down on the table. "I think it's time you took me home." Her heart throbbed like a demon in her breast. She realized that her unresolved anger at her father was at the root of her frustration with Jase, but that didn't help temper her feelings.

When the waitress arrived to try to tempt them with dessert, both she and Jase turned surly looks toward her.

"No," they snapped in unison, sending the flustered woman off to retrieve their check.

She tried one last time. "I wish you'd consider again."

"And I wish you'd be a little more reasonable."

Reba rose, stiff-backed. "I cannot believe you are accusing *me* of being unreasonable." She headed for the door without waiting for him.

At the boat she was about to kick off her pumps and climb aboard when she felt his hands span her waist from behind. Instead of arching back into him as she might have done earlier, she tensed and leaned away.

"Here, let me help you with those deck destroyers before you topple over into the water," he said, coming around to face her. Kneeling on one knee, he slipped a shoe off with an efficient motion. He did the same for the other, but this time his hand remained longer than necessary where he grasped her calf.

A pulse hammered behind her knee, then at her throat. Their eyes met again, and in that moment Reba felt herself weakening. She turned toward the cruiser.

"Hold on a minute. I'll give you an assist." He leaped up the chrome side ladder onto the deck and stretched down a tanned hand.

When he pulled her up to him, their bodies were in close proximity, not quite touching but terribly near. She avoided meeting his eyes while they were so close, knowing that if she did, her resistance to him would melt away. And with Becky's happiness at stake, it was imperative she remain firm.

Not wanting a repeat of their closeness at the controls, she asked if she might sit below during the return trip. He followed her as she stepped down into the bright, spacious interior. The salon was furnished with several large couches upholstered in nautical blue, and paintings of square riggers decorated the walls. She glimpsed several closed doorways. "Are there bedrooms?" she asked, surprised.

"Staterooms," he corrected her.

"Of course, that's what I meant," she returned stiffly. She must sound like an idiot. And what was she doing bringing up the subject of bedrooms, anyway? There was something about Jase's presence that gave even the most innocent thought an erotic edge.

He reached out to caress her arm in a peacemaking gesture. She jerked it away. "Just make yourself comfortable, then," Jase said in a terse tone as he returned to the controls.

Even though he didn't spare the horsepower, it took the better part of an hour to get home, giving Reba a chance to cool down. By the time she helped him tie the lines to the cleats on his U-shaped private dock, she'd regained her composure.

"Would you like to come inside?" Jase asked as they walked up the path to the house. "Becky's still grounded, so I'm certain she'll be here. She'd love to see you."

It was tempting. Reba longed to see Becky and the interior of the house she lived in, but she was equally keen on departing from Jase's company. The day had been too bizarre, first with Jase's romantic overture and then the argument in the restaurant. She felt wrung out, unable to deal with anything more.

"Maybe some other time." She headed straight for the car.

A frown marred his face as he drove her home. Tension filled the air. The brief stabs at conversation were limited to mundane comments on traffic and the problems of commuting from the east side of Lake Washington to downtown Seattle. Reba nearly sighed with relief when at last he pulled into her driveway and parked next to her car.

Jase came around to the passenger side to help her out. Dusk had fallen, shadows concealing them as he turned her into his arms so that his lean face was near, his eyes a blue force, inundating her.

"Come here," he ordered. He pulled her gently but firmly to him, the touch of his strong fingers stirring her flesh through the soft fabric of her dress. As he lowered his mouth to hers, she parted her lips instinctively. His hovered, only a breath away. "You are so special," he whispered. "You're like the sweet-tart candies I loved as a kid. I never could decide which part I enjoyed most." And then his breath entered through her parted lips as flesh met flesh.

She pressed her hands against his chest as if she were trying to protect herself, but she knew she didn't want him to stop. She felt his heartbeat under her palms and his body heat beneath his shirt. Letting her hands slide upward to his taut shoulders, she took in the feel of him through her fingertips. What she discovered there was all male vitality and power. The pressure on her lips ebbed and flowed as his conquered, then released in ever-mounting surges of energy. She yielded to the pressure, and when he retreated, her mouth yearned to feel his once again.

She knew she was making a big mistake. But it didn't matter; his touch washed those thoughts from her mind. Her brain emptied of everything except Jase: his mouth, his broad shoulders under her kneading fingertips, his hard chest against her seeking breasts. In that moment every cell of her body told her that this man was right for her, what she had always needed.

It was Jase who ended the embrace. He smiled down tenderly at her, looking for all the world as if their argument at the restaurant had never occurred. "Do you mind if I use your phone? The car phone's out of order, and I didn't check on Becky while we were at home."

The previous annoyance flared within Reba again. "Don't tell me you watch her night and day."

"Ouch. You *have* judged me harshly, haven't you?" She met his gaze in challenge. "But unfairly?"

"Becky has been looking pale lately, and she seems tired. She might be coming down with something. I wanted to see how she was feeling."

The heat of a guilty flush warmed her cheeks; it served her right to be caught jumping to conclusions. She bowed her head in concession. "Okay, I admit that was a bad call on my part. Of course you can use the phone."

Jase watched Reba digging into her purse for her keys as she walked ahead of him up the porch steps. The cloud cover had thickened, and a brisk wind played havoc with her thick curly brown hair. As he studied her, something warm and sweet washed over him. His heartbeat was very light and fast. He couldn't remember ever feeling quite like this before, even when he first began dating Carolyn. Their relationship had been so different with passive Carolyn agreeing to his every word. Reba possessed more spunk, and with that came a straightforward honesty that he admired. Carolyn had never liked arguments and had gone to great lengths to avoid them. But the peace that gave their household had come with a hefty price; the lack of communication and an inevitable growing apart. Reba was the type of person who tackled problems head-on, and damn the consequences. Not only that, from what he'd seen, her emotions were just as direct. And would her lovemaking follow suit? Oh, Lord, he hoped so.

Reba dropped her keys twice in her purse before she managed to extract them. She'd only just remembered that she'd left the photo album lying open on the coffee table, never imagining at the time that she'd invite Jase inside. Her heart beat in a panicky tempo as she wondered how to spirit the album away before inquisitive Jase saw it.

Thinking fast, she pushed open the door a fraction and then stopped, looking back over her shoulder to Jase. "I have a dog. The backyard fence is broken, and I had to leave her in the house. I'm afraid she might have had an accident. I'll just go in first and check."

Jase's chuckles dismissed the problem. "That's all right. I can handle it."

"No. Really. Bushka is a very large dog. That would be so embarrassing. If you don't mind, just let me look things over first." Without waiting for him to argue further, she slipped inside and pushed the door almost shut, leaving Jase on the porch.

The overgrown dog wriggled with delight at her return and with her huge pink tongue slathered greetings on Reba's hand. "Okay, girl. Enough's enough, already." Reba scrubbed Bushka's head in a quick affectionate hello. Then she darted across the room and snapped up the album. Just as she'd started for the bedroom with it, a gust blew the front door wide open. Bushka barked uncertainly and bounded for the doorway.

Jase stood his ground, staring in amazement as the giant dog, looking for all the world like a yellow grizzly, roared toward him.

"No, girl," Reba commanded her. "Come back here. Sit."

The dog continued as though she were deaf. Jase noted, with relief, that her long shaggy tail was swinging from side to side. He let out a short laugh. "What kind of animal is this?"

"I'm not quite sure. Maybe a little Great Pyrenees. Maybe a little German shepherd. Maybe a little golden retriever."

"You mean a ton of Great Pyrenees."

"I don't know. She was a stray. Since I had a house and lived alone, it seemed like a good idea to invite her to stay." She bestowed a loving smile on the dog. "And I like her company. It's nice to have a warm, living thing around that adores you no matter what."

Jase nodded, agreeing with the sentiment. He liked most animals, and this dog had more than her share of charm. He bent down, holding his hand palm up so that the dog could give it another sniff. A wise precaution, he decided, not wanting to get on the wrong side of a hundred-plus pound animal. As an extra measure, he scratched her behind one floppy ear. She returned his friendliness by jumping up to put her big paws on his chest.

"I'm afraid Bushka isn't very well trained yet." Reba patted her thigh. "Come," Reba ordered her. When Bushka didn't respond she lowered her voice an octave. "I said *come*, and I mean *now!*"

Jase grinned at Reba. "Are you speaking to me?"

"No, not you—" She caught herself and laughed. "Yes, you, too. Come on in."

Jase noticed for the first time that she clutched some sort of large book to her breast. When his eyes met hers, she turned away from him.

"No accidents," he declared as he stepped into the compact living room and shut the door behind him.

After letting the dog out for a moment, Reba excused herself and disappeared down the hallway, giving him a chance to take in the details of her home. Private possessions and the way they were arranged and taken care of spoke volumes about a person's character, Jase believed. His first impression of Reba's home was of warmth. The room was simply furnished but cozy. A colorful patchwork quilt was folded in the corner of a comfortable-looking brown sofa. A pair of blue jogging shoes lay on the floor. On the pine end table a coffee cup embellished with sea gulls rested on a paperback. He lifted the cup and read the title. *Life with Rose Kennedy.* Finally his gaze fell upon an old pine secretary in the corner, displaying a blue pitcher filled with yellow chrysanthemums. The flowers seemed almost like a symbol of the way Reba had come into his life and brightened it.

He spotted a phone on the wall near the kitchen counter and went over to use it. The Norwegian-accented voice of his housekeeper came on the line, assuring him Becky was feeling fine and asking when he would be home for dinner. "Don't worry about me," he said to Ingrid as he noticed Reba padding back into the room minus the large book and shoes. "If I need to, I'll fix something when I get home. I'll probably be late."

He hung up, watching Reba's graceful movements as she filled an automatic coffee maker with water, then retrieved a handful of what looked like homemade chocolate-chip cookies from a panda cookie jar. She set a plate of them on the counter near his elbow.

"Is Becky okay?" she asked.

"Mm-hmm. She's fine." He bit into a fat cookie, discovering it soft and overloaded with chips. Suspecting that everything Reba prepared would taste equally delicious, he wished she would offer to cook dinner for him. Then he realized that it wasn't food he was interested in, but spending more time with her. He longed to stay the evening with her . . . and the night.

It was cool in the house, and Reba put a lighted long-stemmed match to crumpled newspaper beneath the kindling in the red-brick fireplace. Jase finished another cookie before joining her there.

"You're an expert fire starter," he said, coming up behind her and wrapping his arms around her waist the moment she rose to her feet. "You make me feel like bursting into flames whenever I hold you." He leaned his cheek against her luxurious hair and slid his hands up to cup her firm breasts. Her body stiffened, warning him he was pressing too hard, too fast. Although he couldn't bring himself to completely release her, he quickly moved his hands and the conversation to new areas. "Your painting intrigues me," he said, gazing up at the impressionistic work above the fireplace. It was a seascape, dramatically blue. Strong currents were visible under the surface of the water, but the eye was drawn beyond the teeming surf. In the distance a new day dawned on a peaceful sea. It was clear to him what the painting revealed about her. She made such an effort to be self-controlled, but under the smooth surface lay secrets and teeming emotions. Like the ocean, unexpected and even contradictory currents moved with her.

This part of her personality enchanted him. Everything about her enchanted him.

"Reba," he said, his tone forceful, "I want to see you again. I can feel something wonderful happening between us."

Her voice rushed out, gentle and eager. "I'd like to see you again, too."

She began to turn in his arms, and he loosened his grip so that she could face him. Then he was surprised to find her placing her hands on his chest, pushing him away.

Meeting his gaze directly, she said in a tone that brooked no argument, "As soon as Becky is off restriction, we can all go riding together."

"Forget that," he demanded brusquely, folding her into his embrace again. Her smile faded.

"No, Jase. I think—"

It was all the protest she could get out before his mouth came down on hers.

5

THE DOOR SHUT behind Jase with a soft thump, and he heard the safety chain rattle into place. Evidently Reba was putting as impenetrable a barrier between them as possible.

He stood on the front porch. In his left hand he clutched a brown bag containing a half dozen cookies, and in his right he held a Styrofoam cup of steaming coffee, complete with cream.

At that moment the dark clouds overhead decided to unleash the rain they'd held back all day. He took the steps two at a time and jogged toward the car, spilling hot coffee along the way and spilling again as he fumbled with the door handle. By the time he'd managed to get inside, his hair was soaked and his hand was scalded. For some irrational reason the spilt coffee made him furious at Reba.

He sat in the car for a long while, brooding as he stared through the rain-filmed windshield at the cottage where smoke curled from the chimney. He had fully expected to enjoy that fire... and the rest of the evening with Reba. In his mind he went over the scenario he'd assumed he would be experiencing, beginning with a wonderful meal and then moving on to snuggling on her comfortable sofa. They could have talked more. Intrigued by the tantalizing bits of information she'd revealed that afternoon, he'd intended to learn more about her. If she'd grown tired of his curiosity about her personal life, he could have read to her. He'd seen that she owned numerous books, among them one of his favorites, a volume of Mark Twain's short stories. That would have been perfect for a cold and rainy October evening such as this. The rest of the night would have been spent making love. Jase hadn't been able to push the thought from his mind since he'd picked her up that morning. Each time he so much as looked at her, let alone touched her, he felt desire run molten in his veins. Surely she knew how she affected him.

His attention was caught by a shaft of light emerging from the front door. He straightened in his seat. Reba was looking out. So! She'd changed her mind.

Then he saw it.

The black cat ran up the concrete steps and disappeared into the interior glow. With the closing of the door his sudden hope evaporated, leaving what felt like a gaping hole in his chest. The blasted cat!

Jase started the engine with a jerk of his wrist and backed into the street, forcing himself to keep to the speed limit on the neighborhood roads. On the freeway he shook off restraint and sped home. When he finally braked in his garage and killed the engine, he felt an eruption of humor starting in his chest. He tipped his head back and let the laughter come, shaking his head in disbelief.

He was jealous of a cat.

MAX SAT REGALLY UPRIGHT on the kitchen chair next to Reba, his gleaming sapphire eyes following every move of the bagel and lox in her hand. Across the tiny bistro table Debbie leaned forward on bent elbows, her art-fully painted emerald eyes registering interest in every detail of Reba's date with Jase.

"And then he had the nerve to kiss me!" Reba proclaimed in an indignant tone. She stretched her legs out beneath the table and exchanged an expression of disbelief with her friend. "Can you believe the gall of some men?"

Debbie snorted inelegantly. "A man like Jase Kingsford is used to getting his own way. Believe me. I know the type. Bob believes every utterance coming from his mouth is the gospel spoken." With an absent gesture she picked a bit of lox off a plate and offered it to Max, who snatched the morsel from her fingers and made off like a thief. "And if I dare disagree—well, a tumble in bed will bring the silly woman around."

"So what do you do about it?" Reba asked.

"Last time he tried it, I refused to speak to him for a week." She cupped a hand over her mouth, hiding her giggles. "An adolescent thing to do, but effective. I don't think he'll attempt that approach again in the near future. Sometimes actions speak louder than words—or so they say."

"Here, here." Reba lifted her wineglass in agreement to that sentiment. "That was exactly my thinking when I showed Jase the door. He knew I was upset about the way he's treating Becky, but he just wouldn't listen to me. A parent can't force his child into the mold of his own choosing, as if the child is some sort of bland pudding. It's impossible. But that's just what Jase is attempting to do. And he's too blind to see it. He made me so angry that I gave him an ultimatum of sorts, and I suppose that was wrong...but how could he just shrug off what I'd said and then kiss me? Oh!" She shivered in renewed anger. "I've never met such an infuriating man."

"Don't worry about it so much," Debbie advised, flipping her hand in a dismissing gesture. "I've made a point of always telling Bob how I truly feel about things. He never agrees with my opinions and tastes, but after he's had time to think, he often ends up seeing it my way. And Dr. Conservative is as stubborn as they get."

Reba looked out the window into the backyard where Bushka lay snoozing in the late-afternoon sun. She found herself envying the dog's simple life. Recently her own had become dizzyingly complicated. "Bob happens to be in love," she said. "I don't have that power over Jase."

Debbie gave her a sly look over the rim of her glass. "Don't be too sure."

Reba laughed out loud. Jase Kingsford falling in love with her? The notion was so outrageous it was funny. "Give me a break. Jase has his hormones, his heart and his head all well separated."

Debbie was undaunted. "I saw the way he stared at you that day in the hospital. He looked like a man falling in love."

"No. Wrong." Reba drained her glass, the third one since Debbie had arrived that afternoon to carve pumpkins with her. She was tipsy and was enjoying the light-headed sensation. All week she'd felt as though her veins pumped lead instead of blood, and it was a relief to feel some of the weight depart. "He's looking for a little physical action, that's all," she declared.

"So let me get this straight. He made a pass at you, and that's why you kicked him out."

"I asked him to leave," Reba corrected her, "because he had no respect for my opinions."

"And maybe also because he wasn't as easy to manipulate as you'd thought?"

"If he could just see how right I am about Becky's riding," Reba insisted.

"If *you* could just hear how righteous you sound," Debbie returned, the teasing quality in her voice softening the slap of her words.

Reba sank into a sullen slump, not angry with Debbie but weary of the endless circle of their conversation. She stared at the two jack-o'-lanterns on the counter. The next weekend was Halloween, and she and Debbie traditionally brought pumpkins to decorate the childrens' wing. Reba had placed lighted candles in them so that their triangle eyes glittered knowingly.

"Has he called you since then?" Debbie asked.

"No, he hasn't called. I haven't seen Becky at the stable, either." Up to that point she had been able to display a casual front, but now her voice quavered from deep-felt hurt and dismay. "It's been a week. I'm beginning to wonder if I'll ever see either of them again."

"You really care about this guy, don't you?" Debbie's eyes widened at the emotion betrayed by Reba's expression. "And the little girl, too."

"Yes, I do." Part of her wanted to tell all to the sympathetic woman seated across from her, but her father's shame had caused Reba to keep Becky's birth a family secret for so long it felt impossible to speak of now.

A forlorn expression must have descended upon Reba's face, for Debbie spoke quickly as she picked up her purse and stood. "Come with Bob and me tonight. We're going to Franco's Hidden Harbor for dinner. It'll be fun."

Reba shook her head. She appreciated the offer but knew the lovers needed time alone. Besides, an evening of watching those two moon over each other would only dampen her spirits more. "I want to watch *The African Queen* on TV tonight." She put false enthusiasm into her voice. "It's my favorite Humphrey Bogart movie, and I'd hate to miss it."

"Are you sure you don't want to come with us?" Debbie asked, slipping into her coat.

She smiled her appreciation. "Absolutely and positively. I would be heartbroken to miss the show."

Almost immediately after Debbie had gone, Reba wished she'd agreed to go. The house she'd always thought of as a pleasant oasis in a sometimes difficult world now offered her no comfort. Trying to shake off her loneliness, she made busywork in the kitchen, cleaning up the few dishes they'd used and making a fresh pot of coffee. But her mind was filled with thoughts of Debbie, crazy in love and determined to get Bob to the altar. How she envied her friend. For several years she'd yearned to get married and have a family, and at one time had even come close. Yet here she was with no prospective husband in sight. Many of the men she'd dated had been suitable. She'd liked them, and the one she'd nearly married she believed she had loved. But not enough. Or not in the right way. Something always told her there had to be more. The romantic side of her promised that someday a man would come along who would sweep her off her feet, and she was willing to wait for him. But having patience was hard when her heart ached to love.

Unable to find any more tasks to occupy herself, she flopped down on the sofa, pulled the crazy quilt over her stockinged feet and stared at what was left of the fire. The flames curled around the charred wood, soothing her with their bright dance. Jase had liked the fire she'd built, she recalled, the thought of him causing stirrings in the pit of her stomach. She imagined Jase here in her little house, padding across the hardwood floor in sheepskin slippers to stoke the fire into a roaring blaze. Warmth spread through her at the homeyness of the scene. She longed for the fantasy to become reality. Dogs and cats and horses, no matter how much she loved them, could not take the place of a husband and children. If only Jase and Becky could remain in her life.

Reba sat up with a start, shaking the daydreams from her head. It was insane to entertain such notions.

The phone rang and she jumped up to answer it, glad of the distraction. When she heard the sound of Jase's deep voice, she nearly dropped the receiver.

"Hello, Jase." She pressed her hand against her thumping heart.

His chuckles rumbled through the line. "You sound surprised."

"I guess I am," she admitted.

"Are you busy tomorrow?"

Cautiously Reba answered, "Not very. Why?"

"I'd like you to meet Becky and me at the stable."

Reba restrained herself from letting out a whoop of joy. He had relented. "All right. At what time?"

"One o'clock?"

"One is fine with me."

Reba hung up with a song in her heart. One short, simple conversation, and the whole world had changed.

REBA PARKED next to the olive-green Bronco, thankful Jase was still at the stable even though she was a half hour late. Her Volkswagen bug had decided to sleep in that morning, refusing to start until she'd finally worn down the battery. She had been forced to ask a neighbor to help her jump-start it. If she didn't buy a new car soon, she'd be taking the bus to work.

Shoving open the creaky door, she hopped out into the drizzling weather and zipped up her plaid wool jacket against the chill. Though Seattle was blessed with a climate never too hot or too cold, it was also cursed by rain that fell nearly one hundred and fifty days out of the year. But neither her broken-down car nor the damp weather that frizzed her hair could temper Reba's enthusiasm this afternoon.

She headed eagerly into the arena. Inside, her gaze riveted on Jase, and her heart began flip-flopping.

He was holding the reins of a saddled horse, an obese dapple gray that Reba had seen a few times plodding along the trails. All Reba could see of Becky was a pair of jean-clad legs showing between the horse's fat stomach and the ground. She wondered just what was going on.

Reba opened the gate and stepped down from the aisle to the soft dirt, her gaze steady on Jase. As he had every time she saw him, he looked incredibly appealing to her. Today he wore blue jeans again, apparently his favorite attire. The collar of his blue-and-white ski jacket was turned up to hide his strong jawline. On his feet were jogging shoes. She didn't understand why he wasn't wearing boots. Anyone planning to go riding would know enough to put on sturdy footwear. Surely he hadn't changed his mind since the night before.

"Hi, there!" Reba called out as she drew near. "Sorry I'm late."

Jase's gaze was the first to greet her, and at once she forgot the cold as his smile heated her. His eyes devoured her, and she stared back at him with an unmistakable glow of her own. Stunned and unnerved by the intensity of her joy at seeing him again, Reba was glad when Becky bounded out from behind the horse to interrupt the intimate exchange.

"Reba! I thought you'd never get here," she said, coming around the tail end of the horse and bouncing from one foot to the other like an overexcited puppy. "You'll never guess what Dad is going to do."

Reba flicked a questioning look to Jase, who appeared altogether too pleased with himself. "He's going riding with us?"

"No!" Laughter spilled through Becky's words. "Even neater than that. He's buying me a horse!" She patted the gray with enthusiasm. "Maybe this one."

Surprised by Becky's announcement, Reba didn't know what to say. It didn't take long for her to realize that this was a natural turn of events. Jase was not a man to waffle over decisions, or to go about life in a halfhearted manner. Either he would forbid Becky from riding altogether, or he would endorse riding by purchasing a horse for her. Her admiration for him took a giant leap forward.

"It's true," he said, his eyes continuing to smile at her although his voice had become serious. "I thought about what you said about being fair and about the dangers of being overprotective. It made me furious at the time because you'd hit the nail so squarely on the head. I wanted to protect my daughter. I couldn't see past that. You forced me to see that I was smothering her." He glanced down at Becky, who beamed up adoringly at him. Reba knew her own gaze was similar, and she couldn't help it.

Becky stroked the horse's broad head. "I do wish Ghost were younger, but he'll be okay, I guess. Having my own horse will be the greatest."

Reba gave the ancient specimen of horseflesh before her a critical once-over. Ghost was oblivious to the activity and noise of the arena, busy with a dozen or more riders. The gelding stood with a back hoof cocked, and his eyelids drooping as though he were falling asleep then and there. With Becky's strong desire for a horse she would be grateful for anything standing on four legs, Reba thought in distress. Somehow she must convince Jase this wasn't the type of horse an experienced rider such as Becky would be happy with for long, regardless of her jubilant spirits of the moment.

Quite suddenly an idea came to her mind. Her eyes flashed with excitement. "Jase, I have a wonderful solution."

He rubbed a knuckle against his dark blond mustache, eyeing her with suspicion. "I wasn't aware there was a problem."

"Well, there is. And it's a major one. This horse isn't right for Becky."

He studied the horse, taking pains to walk all the way around in thorough examination, and came to stand beside Reba. She suspected he had done so to be near her. He rested a fist on either hip, causing his jacket to bunch and make his chest appear even broader than it was. "This animal is perfect. He's calm, good-tempered, broken in."

"Broken-down, you mean," Reba challenged in a soft voice. She nodded toward a group of young girls who were riding their horses over the jumps that lined the center of the arena. "Becky's going to want to jump, to ride in competitions like her friends do. This old beast won't be able to stand that pace. You'd be keeping Becky from half the fun of owning a horse." Sensing Jase was on the point of making a decision, she continued. "I think the answer is for you to buy Amber from me." Two sets of surprised eyes stared at her. She rushed on. "You see, I bought Amber on an impulse before I thought about such mundane realities as budgets. I desperately need a new car, but I'll never be able to afford one as long as I'm paying for boarding. It was a mistake to buy Amber, but now I love her dearly, and it would be a relief to see her to go to someone as nice as Becky."

"But, Reba," Becky said, confusion and gratitude mixing in her voice, "You won't have a horse to ride then."

"Sure I will. If I take riding lessons here, I can rent the stable's school horses to take out on the trails."

"Whoa." Jase held up a hand to halt the conversation, and sliced a look to Reba that doused her rising excitement. "Things are getting out of hand. I've already agreed to buy this gray horse. I think it might be safer to go with the one that's tried and true."

"Why don't you watch Becky ride Amber before you make a selection," she persisted. "You're a reasonable man. Can't you agree to that much?"

Jase resented Reba's exasperating way of stirring up trouble, and yet he knew she'd been right before. She'd forced him to realize the error not letting Becky ride would have been. He must not allow his strong protective instincts to overshadow his good sense again. "All right," he said between clenched teeth. "Go get the mare and we'll have a look."

With a shout and a jump Becky raced out of the arena to fetch Amber. Even though many riders were using the enclosed area, Reba felt very much alone with Jase. He didn't attempt to touch or kiss her in this public place, but instead caressed her with the sensual look in his eyes.

"I've missed you," he said, the deep timbre of his voice underlining the sincerity of those simple words. "More than I ever thought I would."

Reba inhaled a shaky breath, her lungs filling not only with the horse-scented arena air, but also with the spicy aroma of his after-shave. All of her senses sharpened when she was near him. She responded to the slightest stimuli: the briefest glance, the subtlest change in the tone of his voice, the most delicate tracing of his warm breath on her skin. It made her extremely uncomfortable, this hypersensitivity, yet she never wanted it to end.

Reba soaked in his presence, trying to make up for the week they were apart. There was also a matter she felt she had to clear up. "Last week, when I told you I would only see you if we all went riding together, I didn't mean it to sound like blackmail." She rubbed her forehead. "That sounds so conceited! I just want you to know I would have wanted to see you again regardless of what you'd decided to do." She smiled up at him, her eyes filled with the joy she was feeling. "Although I have to admit, I'm delighted about how things have turned out."

He brushed a strand of hair from her forehead, as though he couldn't resist making some physical contact with her. "I'm glad to hear that. Even though that aspect did cross my mind, it wouldn't have kept me from you for long. I've needed someone like you to shake me up a bit."

Reba laughed, glad her confession was over with and feeling generous. "I think you try very hard to be a good parent. I can see what an understanding man you are."

"Better save your judgment until the outcome of this horse-buying business. You might have to take something back."

"I know you'll make the right decision. You haven't failed me yet."

Becky had entered the arena on Amber, and seeing the two of them together reaffirmed Reba's original opinion. The purebred lines of the mare and the delicately built girl were in perfect proportion, and it was obvious the horse responded to every cue Becky gave her. Jase watched with an intense expression on his face as Becky put the mare through her paces.

"Well, Jase," Reba said when Becky brought Amber to a stop before them. "What do you think?"

He stroked his mustache again, this time plainly for dramatic effect. "I've decided to buy this mare—"

Becky let out an excited cry, forcing Jase to continue in a louder voice. "On one condition. That Reba rides with you for the next month. I haven't been convinced that you can handle this animal as well as you think, the incident at the show grounds proving my point. If Reba agrees to watch over you at least that long, then yes, the horse is yours."

Becky's squeals of delight had every head in the arena turning toward them. Reba didn't need to think it over; at once she agreed.

Becky scrambled down from the saddle and threw herself into her father's arms, shouting thank-yous and squeezing him. Warmth surged up from Reba's heart at the touching scene. If only she had the right to join in the hugging.

Becky released her father's waist and turned to Reba, launching into a flurry of planning, when and where to ride together.

Jase sighed, loudly enough to get their attention. "I suppose I'll have to buy the saddle and bridle, too."

"Of course, Dad," Becky said, her face now serious.

"And just what else will I have to fork out for?" he asked with fake severity. "Gold-plated horseshoes?"

Jase's eyes filled with the hopelessness of a man resigned to an uncertain future, at which Becky exploded into giggles. How wrong she had been to think of him as unreasonable, Reba mused. He was wonderful. Simply wonderful. If she didn't watch herself, he would steal her heart.

"I think the prospective check-writer should try the horse for himself." Reba's grin openly dared Jase.

He backed away, waving his hands in a cross of refusal. "Forget it, gals. You can go find your laughs elsewhere."

"You've never ridden before, have you?" Reba asked.

"I don't intend to start now."

"Oh, pleeease," Becky begged.

"Go on, Jase," Reba urged. "You might even enjoy it. Besides, it's only fair. After all, I went along with piloting the boat, didn't I?" Without waiting for Jase's reply, she turned and began to let down the stirrup leathers to accommodate his longer legs. "Well?" She adjusted the opposite stirrup. "Give it a try?"

"Oh, hell, why not? Live dangerously, I always say."

Admiration for him tingled inside Reba; it took a big man to risk looking foolish. Keeping her face perfectly straight, she showed him how to place his foot in the stirrup and grasp the cantle of the saddle to mount. Once he was astride, she stepped back to study his seat.

"You look good on a horse," she said, partly to encourage him, partly because it was the truth. His long, athletic legs gently gripped Amber's sides, and he held the reins firmly, without pulling her tender mouth. He was tense but unafraid. Reba knew he could be an expert horseman if he cared to.

"I know the basics from watching Becky's first classes." He nudged Amber with his heels and broke into a wicked grin. "I'll just get warmed up for some jumps. Why don't you raise them a few feet?" he wisecracked.

Smiling, Reba leaned back against the fence and watched Jase walk Amber around the ring. Ghost stood off to one side, held by Becky. Reba draped an arm across Becky's shoulders and hugged her, luxuriating in her daughter's happiness and her own. Being here with Becky and Jase gave Reba a sense of wholeness she'd never felt before. In her joy she ignored the deep inner voice that warned her to be careful; she didn't want to be reminded that she had no right to be here.

With more skill than Reba had expected, Jase rode back to them at a swift trot, bringing the mare to a smooth halt a few feet away. He grinned, and like a cowboy too long in the saddle, dismounted and swaggered over to them. "This mare will do, I guess." He tossed the reins to Becky, who at once reset the stirrup length and rode off to display Amber to her friends.

Alone again, Jase wrapped an arm around Reba's waist and drew her close. His eyes held a seductive gleam. "To get even with you for badgering me into that ride, I've decided to change the terms of our agreement."

"What! I already told you I'd ride with Becky for the next month."

With one hand he rubbed the seat of his jeans. "I might not be able to sit down for a week. Is that fair?"

Reba couldn't hold in her chuckles. "Okay, shoot. What am I going to have to do?"

He pulled her even nearer to him and placed a light kiss on her mouth that she felt all the way to her knees. "For starters, go to lunch with me today. Then dinner tonight. I'd like to see you this coming week, too. We'll car shop. Finally I want you to come to my house next weekend for Halloween night. Becky's going to an overnight party, so we'll have the haunted mansion to ourselves."

Reba shivered excitedly at the implications of that.

Jase continued to hold her while her emotions raged war, and when his fingers moved up to stroke her cheek, she knew she was gone. She smiled up at him, her surrender visible in her eyes.

"You don't want a lot, do you?"

"Nothing but it all," he answered. "Nothing but all of you, sweet Reba."

6

NERVOUS ANTICIPATION knotted Reba's stomach as she drove her new white Mustang down the Kingsford driveway, defined by small night-lights as it curved toward the lake. At her first sight of the five dormers outlined against a full Halloween moon, Jase's words of invitation came back to her. *We'll have the haunted mansion to ourselves.*

The chill tickling her spine had nothing to do with fear of ghosts that might be out this night. Her sense of apprehension came from knowing each passing day brought her closer to deep involvement with Jase Kingsford.

The past week had been wonderful. Too wonderful, she thought as she stopped the Mustang in the broad parking area in front of the house. She'd ridden with Becky, gone shopping with Jase for her new car and shared an expedition with father and daughter for Becky's new riding boots. Every time they were together, she found Jase more irresistible, but until tonight there had been little opportunity for them to be alone. Now, as she walked toward the beautiful traditional home, with its gnarled old wisteria vine twisting over the front entry and jack-o'-lanterns guarding the door, she felt excitement race through her.

She had just raised her hand to ring the bell when one of the double doors flew open and a sturdy woman, her gray hair tied back in a neat bun, filled the doorway.

"Oof!" she exclaimed, a startled expression on her face as she clutched her overnight satchel to her breast and stepped backward. "I was yust coming out. Did you knock?"

"I was just about to. I'm Reba McCallister. Mr. Kingsford is expecting me."

Enthusiasm replaced surprise on her face, and she gestured for Reba to come inside. "Ya, sure. Come in, please. Mr. Kingsford, he told me he was expecting a very important person." The large-boned woman smiled at Reba, who stepped into the parquet-floored entry hall. "It is for you that all that mess is going on in my kitchen. Mr. Kingsford is cooking."

"Reba." Jase called out from somewhere behind the woman, whose heavy black coat blocked Reba's view. At the welcoming ring in his deep voice something caught at her vitals, but she managed to keep her features composed.

The big woman, her expression pleased but respectful, turned toward her employer. "It's your guest, Mr. Kingsford."

With her first glimpse of Jase's smiling face, Reba's blood began to pound in her ears. His navy cashmere sweater was dusted with flour, and he was wiping his hands on an apron tied around his slim waist. This display of domesticity was the last thing she'd expected.

"You and Ingrid have met?" he asked, unable to keep the telltale softness from his voice as he drank in the sight of Reba slipping off her coat to reveal a vermilion silk blouse and matching slacks. Caressing her neck was a strand of cultured pearls that she fingered nervously.

"We was just meeting." The Scandinavian woman beamed at Reba. "I'm Mr. Kingsford's housekeeper." A knowing look came to Ingrid's eyes as she glanced from Reba's flushed cheeks to Jase's intense gaze. "You two have a lovely time this evening. I got to get going now. I told my daughter I would be at her house in time for dinner. Don't forget, Mr. Kingsford, my special salad dressing is in the refrigerator door." She gave Reba one last long interested look and, as if she approved of her, a sincere parting smile. "Good night, Miss Mc-Callister."

Although they'd gone shopping just the day before, as soon as the door closed behind Ingrid, Jase hauled Reba into his arms as eagerly as if he hadn't seen her for months. He crushed her to him, taking her mouth by storm. Reba was breathless by the time Jase released her lips.

"You're early," he said. "I'm glad. I've decided I'd like to spend as much time with you as possible. You have me bewitched. I hope you realize that."

Her heart lodged in her throat. Had he fallen in love with her? She didn't know. She couldn't tell. His words could be interpreted many ways. Tears began to burn at the back of her eyes, so overwhelmed and confused was she by her feelings. "Jase, I . . . I don't know what to say."

He cupped her chin, lifting it so that she had no choice but show him her misted eyes. "What's this? Do I drive you to tears?"

She smiled and shook her head. "I have something in my eye." It was an outright lie, and she knew she wasn't fooling him. Needing a moment to collect herself, she stepped back and out of his embrace, then handed her coat to Jase to put away. "Are we alone?" Reba glanced over her shoulder, half expecting to see Becky.

"It's just the two of us and the goblins here." His gaze bore into hers with an intimacy that took her breath away. "Is it all right?" he asked in a soft and tender tone. "We can still call this off if you want to."

Mixed emotions surged through her. If he'd come close to falling in love with her, she surely teetered on the very brink. The yearning in her heart pushed her one direction while the fears in the back of her mind pushed her in another. Blocking out the clamoring of her doubts, Reba took the plunge, heart and mind.

"I'll stay," she said simply.

"Well!" A heavy sigh rode on the end of his exclamation. "You had me worried there for a moment."

Feeling in a love-dazed state, Reba let Jase take her hand and lead her down the central hallway into a large kitchen with adjoining family room where a massive river-rock fireplace contained a bright fire. "I thought we'd have dinner in here. This is where Becky and I have our meals," he said, indicating a table set for two in front of the roaring blaze. Through the doorway at the other end of the kitchen Reba could see a sparkling chandelier and gleaming mahogany table. "I usually entertain at restaurants. We haven't used the formal dining room since we moved in. I'm hoping you'll help Becky and me bring the room alive for Thanksgiving. If you were here, it would be like one of the wonderful holiday dinners I remember."

A sweet poignancy caught at her emotions. As much as she longed to be included in the Kingsford family, she knew she'd better slow down on making plans with Jase. A brief affair—not a future—was the most she could share with him.

"I'd like to, but I always visit my father on holidays." She spit out the hasty fib, then hid her shame by turning away from his perceptive gaze. Noticing four mysterious flour-coated patties on the countertop, she changed the conversation to a less disturbing topic. "What's for dinner?" she asked, going over to a breadboard where a mound of crushed crackers rested. In the extra vegetable sink at least five different kinds of greens floated, looking succulent and fresh.

He made a sweeping gesture of presentation. "The entrée is that rare and wondrous shellfish, Puget Sound abalone."

"Oh, how marvelous! Where did you get it? I thought abalone was impossible to come by anymore."

"It is. Between the seals and the sea otters, there are practically none left in the Sound." He joined her at the counter and finished rolling the crumbs to bread the seafood. "But I have my resources."

Reba raised her brows, chuckling. "What? Some out-of-the-way little fish market?"

"No, a secret cove." He grinned with the pride of the true male provider. "I dove for them last summer and froze them. I might just teach you to dive next year and take you to my special spot." He cocked his head and studied her with a teasing gleam in his eye. "If you can be trusted."

"I suppose I'd have to take a solemn oath."

"No," he said, laughing. He finished coating the abalone and washed and dried his hands. Without warning he drew her to him, his expression serious despite the curve of his mouth. "I do trust you, you know." The velvet tones of his voice stroked her nerves.

Reba tried to swallow her extreme discomfort and made a sickly attempt at smiling. "You sound very sure of me."

"There is something mysterious about you, something in your face I can't quite read. Do you have a deep dark secret, Reba McCallister?"

She suppressed the guilt that throbbed in her breast. "Yes," she said, making another valiant effort to smile. "Yes, I do. The secret is that I'm starved. And I'm beginning to think feeding me is the last thing on your mind."

He sighed. "I admit my thoughts aren't completely on dinner." Bending forward, he kissed her on the forehead before skimming his lips down the trail of her nose to her mouth. There he lingered, melting her bones with a kiss that promised even better to come.

Reba knew that if she didn't take control of the situation, they'd end up in bed before they managed to eat a bite. Although her body was more than ready for Jase's lovemaking, her mind wasn't. She felt uptight and jittery, ashamed of the false front she'd presented to this honest man. He deserved better than she could give. She gazed into his eyes, longing to find in those deep blue seas a resolution to her anguish. But they held only a churning desire that made her feel weaker.

With great effort she withdrew from him. "I think I'd better help with dinner. We can't continue like this."

He nodded in agreement, albeit reluctantly. "You're right, sensible Reba."

"I'm glad you see it my way." She gathered up the salad makings, and Jase handed her a large wooden bowl.

"It's already rubbed with salt and garlic. The dressing is in—"

"The refrigerator," Reba completed, feeling more relaxed with the small distance between them.

Jase's rich laughter floated over to her. "Ingrid knows all about you, of course. Becky talks about you constantly. When I told Ingrid I'd invited you over, I never saw her so excited. If she'd had her way, she would have prepared a grand dinner and then waited on us hand and foot. The extent of my culinary expertise is assembling sandwiches, so you understand her concern. She feared my interpretation of a three-course meal might scare you off."

"Three courses," Reba echoed in a rush, ignoring all else. "There's salad and abalone. What's the third?"

He opened one of the oven doors in the wall, eyes alight with pride as he pulled out a magnificent golden-brown loaf. "Bread."

The meal was delicious. Not able to eat another bite, Reba laid her fork on her plate and sighed in contentment. She was terribly flattered that he'd gone to so much trouble for her. The abalone, he'd told her over dinner, was the last of his limited supply. He'd been saving it for a very special occasion.

"The abalone was fantastic," she said as she finished her wine. "Another triumph as the result of your daredevil sporting life."

"Risk does have its rewards." The seductiveness of his hooded gaze told her he referred to more than just sport.

Reba looked away, not wanting to begin a discussion of their relationship. Glancing around the richly paneled family room, she noticed a collage of snapshots of Becky. "Were you the photographer?" she asked.

He nodded. "Photography comes in very handy to a journalist." He smiled as he studied the pictures. "And I was one of those dads who, right from the start, had to have a memory of every moment of his child's life." He glanced at Reba. "Becky's adopted, you know. Or did you?"

"She mentioned it just a few days ago."

"You see, Carolyn and I had wanted a child for a long time. When it was discovered that she couldn't have children, we immediately decided to adopt. It took a long time, but finally we were told there was a child. The mother had asked that the baby keep her given name, Rebecca Marie. I'll never forget the first moment I saw my beautiful little girl. One look and I lost my heart."

"With your coloring so much the same, you could have easily passed her off as your own."

"She *is* my own," he said. "And I feel that keeping the truth from her would have been wrong. That she's adopted is unimportant. I've always emphasized that she was meant to be a Kingsford, and that I'm proud to be her father."

Jase spoke with such forthright conviction that Reba felt the strength of his words just as she knew Becky must. "Are you ever worried Becky's natural parents might find her?" Reba asked.

"I know it's irrational, but yes, I do. Especially now. Becky's going through a difficult time with her mother gone. She's vulnerable. I don't know what she might do if her birth mother turned up at this point."

Knowing Jase considered losing Becky a real possibility curtailed any notions Reba had about revealing her identity. No matter how much she assured him she would not try to take his daughter, he would always be worried. It was better she keep her secret and spare him the anxiety.

Reba rose from her chair a little unsteadily and began gathering up the dishes. Jase was at once by her side, halting her hand with his.

"Leave the dishes." He bent to tease her ear with tiny kisses. "My guests aren't required to do the washing up."

"How about a tour of the house, then?" Her body quivered from the nearness of his. She edged away, only to have him capture her hand in his again.

"I'll bet you'd like to see Becky's room."

"You don't think she'd mind, do you?"

"She might object if it were anyone else, but not you." His eyes were warm on Reba's face as he led her out of the room and up the winding staircase.

Becky's room was a delight. The color scheme was Wedgwood blue and white, the ruffled bedspread matching the charming floral print covering the walls. Dozens of bears, many dressed in elaborate outfits, lounged on the bed and the cozy window seat. Reba released Jase's hand and turned in a circle to take it all in, wanting to commit every inch of the room to memory. As she turned back to him, she saw on the night-stand a silver-framed portrait. In it an attractive woman smiled up at her. Reba picked up the picture.

"Is this Carolyn?"

He nodded. "That photo was taken only a few weeks before the accident."

"Accident?" Reba had never asked how Jase's wife had died. "Was she killed in an auto accident?"

"No." He looked at Reba in surprise, frowning. "I thought you knew. I assumed Becky had told you." He glanced away, his forehead creased as though he were puzzling something out. "No. I should have realized she wouldn't. She hasn't been able to talk about her mother."

Reba waited for him to continue.

"Carolyn's family owns a horse farm in Virginia," he explained. "Fox hunting is the local sport, and Carolyn loved it. She was killed during a hunt when her horse missed a jump and threw her."

"Oh, Jase. I had no idea." At last she understood. "No wonder you were so concerned about Becky's riding. You must have thought I was extremely unfeeling for wanting Becky to have a spirited horse."

"I could never think of you as being unfeeling. You were absolutely right. There's risk inherent in almost every sport. By making an issue out of her riding, I caused her to focus more on her mother's death." He paused, rubbing his mustache thoughtfully. "There's already been a difference since I yielded and bought Amber for her. The tension between us is gone, and I haven't heard a fib all week. You know, I had been ready to take her to a counselor. But maybe I'll hold off on that. Maybe Becky can let go of her mother's death now and move on with her life."

Reba set the picture down. "I'm glad, Jase," she murmured, her heart swelling with admiration for him. He was an exemplary father, and Becky lived a wonderful life. There was no excuse to continue investigating her daughter's world.

Now, she told herself. *Now* was the time for her to make her exit while she still could. But even as she told herself this, Jase reached over to trail a light touch down her arm that entranced her tongue and limbs. She was conscious of a tight, almost painful catch of the heart. She averted her eyes, fearing they would reveal all: her blatant desire, her need to love, her secrets.

"Come on," Jase said, breaking the spell. "I'll show you where I work at home."

Taking her elbow, he escorted her down the hallway and into a study dominated by a huge oak desk. Among the piles of important-looking papers sat a rough clay pencil holder obviously shaped by young fingers and a humorous plastic figurine entitled World's Greatest Dad. Reba's gaze flicked to an antique trunk pushed up against one side of the desk. A swatch of glittery red fabric dangled out.

Jase reached down and opened the lid. A tangle of colorful clothes filled the box. "Becky dragged the old family costume box out of the attic and was trying to get my opinion of what she should wear to Heather's costume party tonight."

"I'll bet she dressed as a princess," Reba said, smiling dreamily at her vision of Becky resplendent in a ruffled gown and jewels. "I could just see her in a pink silk dress and diamond tiara."

Jase glanced at her, amused. "Try mud-splattered riding boots and goggles."

"What?"

"She went as a jockey."

Reba laughed, rolling her eyes heavenward. "I should have guessed. Becky isn't exactly the delicate princess type. Unless these days royal young ladies like to wear jeans and muck out horse stalls."

Though they continued to talk about the girls' party, Reba sensed Jase's thought were far from children's games. With each passing minute the sexual tension between them increased, until she felt consumed by a need for him that seemed to spring from her very core.

Trying to distract herself, Reba picked up the red fabric spilling out of the trunk. It was a flamboyant gypsy skirt. She held it against her waist. "This is gorgeous. What goes with it?" She dug further into the box. "Look at this! George and Martha Washington costumes."

Jase picked up the white George Washington wig. "I remember my dad wearing this when I was ten. He was so straitlaced and father-of-our-country-looking that the costume suited him."

"Try it on," Reba requested with a fun-loving gleam in her eye and childlike excitement in her voice. "Let's see what you look like."

He complied, adjusting the white wig around his ears. "What do you think?" He placed one foot on top of the trunk and assumed the posture of George Washington crossing the Delaware.

She laughed. "George didn't have a mustache, but there's something right about you in that pose. Maybe it's your far-seeing blue eyes."

"No. There's something else I have in common with old George. Don't you know what that is?"

"Wooden teeth?"

"No." He continued to smile at her, his teeth even and white, but his eyes had become sober. "I cannot tell a lie, Reba. I'm crazy about you." He held up his hand in a solemn pledge. "And that's the honest truth."

His words again reminded her of the lies that had brought her here. She promised herself that as soon as this month that she'd agreed to ride with Becky was finished, she would part from the lives of the Kingsfords. She had no choice but to walk away from the daughter she loved and the man she desired.

Jase was waiting for her response, but she turned away and continued examining the contents of the costume box. She tried to make her voice light as she held up a scoop-necked satin blouse with flowing sleeves. "Look, I've found the rest of the gypsy outfit."

"Try it on. I'd like to see you as a gypsy. You'll be perfect with your dark hair and eyes."

Jase showed her to the master bedroom and left her there to change. While Reba donned the outfit, she scanned the spacious room. It was filled with glossy, expensive-looking Chippendale furniture that had probably belonged to his parents when they'd lived here. The wall that faced the lake was almost all window, and with the full moon and stars lighting the night Reba felt as though she were on a ship at sea, alone with the sky and the water.

A knock on the door preceded Jase's voice. "Are you ready?"

At her signal he entered. She burst into laughter at the sight of him.

He swaggered over to her, looking ridiculous and yet very masculine in his baggy shirt and ragged pantaloons. He'd tied a red handkerchief around his head and wore a black patch over one eye. "Come here, my pretty. This pirate has plans for ye."

"Oh, no!" she squealed, retreating backward step by step until the barrier of the bed against her legs halted her escape.

"Trapped, ye are." He flicked off the lamp before closing the distance between them with one last step and gathering her into his powerful embrace.

His mouth descended upon hers, silencing any protest she might have wanted to make. But Reba made no struggle. Instead, she arched unprotestingly against his body, marveling at how warm and gentle and tough he was. She yielded her mouth to his demanding kiss and clutched his strong neck, knowing that it was this she'd been waiting for all evening. She drew him to her and moved her hands upward so that her fingers could comb through his fair hair. The pirate scarf fell and the eye patch became dislodged as she caressed the finely textured strands with her fingertips.

She pressed her lips to his, noting the feel of his mustache, its exciting silky roughness. With increasing pressure he probed her mouth with his tongue, plundering every space within. His kiss awakened fully the aching desire she'd so long suppressed.

Jase finally broke away, his labored breath against her earlobe. "Before we go any further . . . are you protected, darling?" When Reba whispered her positive reply, he released a sigh of relief. "Good. I want you so badly. It would be hell to stop now." He lowered his lips to her throat, his mustache brushing her skin with soft, seductive ripples. "I'm going to make love to you."

It was a statement, quiet and true. He wasn't asking for her permission, and for that she was glad. Much as she needed him, needed to give herself to him, she wanted their lovemaking simply to happen. She wanted to be possessed by this intrepid pirate.

Not waiting for her response, he lowered her lips to hers. She submitted to her uncontrollable longing by digging her short nails into the firm flesh of his back and pressing her pliant body even closer to his. He slid his hands down to encompass her hips, lowering the point where their bodies made most intense contact. No further words were needed to express his hard need for her femininity. Deep within her female center, passion like a hot spring burst forth, flowing into her veins and washing away the last of her caution.

Jase groaned with deep-throated pleasure, kneading her buttocks, anchoring himself against her warmth. "It's too good," he muttered hoarsely. "Too good to be believed."

The next thing Reba knew, she was lying back on the bed with Jase slowly coming down on top to press her into the mattress. While he caressed her mouth with his, he moved his hands along the curves of her body as if he knew them well from having made love to her a thousand times before. He pulled the blouse from the band of the skirt and slid his fingers onto her trembling skin, releasing the catch of her bra. She shifted slightly, helping him slip the blouse over her head and the bra free from her shoulders. Tenderly he traced the swell of her firm breasts before cupping both as if claiming them to be his. With each thumb he tantalized an aching nipple, and when his greedy lips discovered the hard little nubs, she moaned from the exquisite sensation.

At the sound he released her and chuckled, a soft low pirate laugh. "The wanton gypsy no longer wishes to escape?"

Reba's face heated with a blush. "You're embarrassing me," she murmured.

He returned his mouth to hers, holding her tongue with his to still her protests. With a sensitive touch he explored beneath her skirt to seek the point of her greatest pleasure, and she forgot her shyness. As he stroked her, she nearly went out of her mind with pleasure. She writhed and heard herself making small sounds, half cries, as her desire grew to an unbearable level.

"Sweet Reba," he said. "I've been crazy with wanting you these last weeks. I can't wait any longer."

When he withdrew his hand, she sucked in panting breaths in an attempt to restore her sanity. He left the bed to remove his clothes, tossing them onto the floor in his haste. Reba's followed, and they took a moment to study each other's nude bodies, opalescent in the moonlight.

"You're a picture," he said, at last joining her on the bed. Capitulating to his light touch, she lay back. He leaned over her, brushing the hair from her cheek and then kissing her nose. "I'm in love," he said softly. "I'm sure of it."

And I. Her heart pounded out the beat of the words. *In love. In love.* She reached for his body and began to explore his firm belly with her fingers, stroking the fine wash of short blond hairs that spilled wider to surround swollen maleness. There she touched him intimately.

He groaned with pleasure. "Reba, honey, I can't take any more of this." He moved over her, and their mouths joined. Though she could sense the impatience of his need, he slowed and gentled his movements as he nudged her knees apart and settled himself between her thighs. The fit was so right, so beautiful that the last of Reba's doubts washed away. All of her being focused on the sensations Jase created with his desire, she instinctively raised her hips and found herself begging, "Now, please! Oh, Jase!"

He entered her with the smooth power of a breaking wave. With a cry of ecstasy she gave herself, riding the wild pounding surf with him, clutching to him in their sea of passion. As his plunging grew stronger and deeper, her body seemed to take on a life of its own, arching in Jase's every thrust in uninhibited response. They were caught up in a storm wave that crested endlessly, finally breaking with shattering force, and she was filled, completed, made whole as he poured himself into her.

For a long time they lay spent, hot, moist bodies entwined, lovers washed up together, basking on a warm, peaceful shore. Finally Reba drew in a shivery, disbelieving breath and opened her eyes to the large shadowed form that still cradled her tightly against him. Her passion had gone beyond anything she'd known before, leaving her body quivery and her thoughts jumbled. She listened to his now-steady breathing, wondering about the incredible experience they'd just shared. It was hard to imagine lovemaking bringing more joy than this.

Not quite ready to let reality invade her bliss, she let her eyelids drift closed and nestled her head into the curve of Jase's broad shoulder.

He traced a finger gently across her mouth, brushing away strands that had caught in the corner of her lips. She sighed drowsily. "You're not drifting away from me, are you?" he asked, then pulled her closer to him as if assuring his possession.

"What if I did? Would you be upset?" She smiled, but her eyelids were too heavy to open.

"Damn right I would. Now that I've got you in my clutches, I don't intend to let you escape. Not even into sleep."

"You are demanding." She opened her eyes with reluctance, but already felt the renewed stirrings of desire. Rising on an elbow, she pressed a kiss against his muscular chest, barely sprinkled with soft hair that was invisible in the moonlight.

"Yes, I guess I am demanding." He caressed her body, beginning his journey at her rib cage, indenting at her slim waist and continuing to the feminine swell of her hips. It was as though he were noting the dimensions of his newly claimed territory. "And I'm very thorough. When I go after something, I learn everything I can about it." With a powerful sweep he flung her atop his sprawled body. "By the time I'm through, I'm going to know everything about you."

7

REBA WOKE AND DREW IN a sleepy breath, her first conscious perception the musky scent of Jase's chest beneath her cheek. No perfume could have smelled more wonderful to her.

She lay without opening her eyes or stirring. Her thoughts were coated in a warm fuzzy haze of contentment, and her soul vibrated with joy.

"Reba?" Jase's deep voice was thick with slumber.

"Yes?"

"Did you wake me up?"

"No."

"I must have been dreaming, then."

He didn't say more, and after a long moment Reba lifted her chin to see that his eyes were closed as if he'd fallen back asleep. She wondered if he'd drifted off.

"About what?" she asked, now fully awake and intrigued by his dream.

"Mmm." He sounded barely conscious, but then she noticed the twitch of a muscle in his jaw. She rose on her right elbow, peered down at his face and made a bold guess. "It must have been a sex dream."

His eyelids flew open.

"Aha!" she said. "I thought so."

All trace of sleepiness vanished as he curled the edges of his mouth into a smile both teasing and sensual. "How did you guess?" He wrapped an arm around her waist and pulled her partly on top of him. "I was dreaming about this dark-haired, dark-eyed woman. A wild, wanton creature...insatiable, really." He stared at the ceiling with a puzzled expression. "Now who could that have been?"

"Someone you know?"

"In a way we'd come to know each other, well, intimately."

With her index finger Reba traced circles around his bronze nipple. "I see," she said thoughtfully. "So you and this dark-haired woman were intimate strangers."

He nodded, his smile fading. "I kept having the feeling she would vanish." He turned his ocean-blue eyes to her. "Of course, dream women are like that, aren't they? One day you wake up and they're gone."

Reba shrugged. "And that bothers you?"

"Yes."

"A great deal?"

"A great deal."

Her heart lodged in her throat, keeping her from replying. She laid her dizzy head on his shoulder, trying to come to grips with the import of his words. He began to caress her with long, lazy strokes from the center of her back to her thigh. Desire spread through her body and mind, honing her senses and dulling her raging thoughts. Responding out of instinct, she arched into him and purred under her breath.

Although she'd reveled in the aggressive behavior Jase had displayed the evening before when their barely leashed passion had dictated the intensity of their union, this morning she wanted to set a slower pace. When Jase started to rise on an elbow, she placed her palms on his chest and gently halted him. Yielding to her touch, he allowed himself to be pushed back down onto the bed. His brow wrinkled in curiosity, but when she leaned over and kissed him, he moaned in delight, a low guttural sound that sent tingles rippling through her.

All around them milky morning light coated the room, obscuring sharp angles and muting colors. The central heating came on, its hum the only sound beside the rustle of the sheets and the quickening rhythm of their breathing. Reba moaned and pulled Jase closer. Sensing what she wanted, he shifted her onto her back and beneath his crouched body. Hovering above her, he waited for her to make the next move. He stared deeply into her eyes with a gaze so fiercely loving it took her breath away. When she thought she could not stand one second more of waiting, she grasped his firm waist and lowered him to her. The instant he entered her, she lost herself in the sensation of being joined to him. It was such excruciating sweetness that everything else was closed out of her world.

But later, when Reba awoke for the second time that morning, her old fears returned. Jase lay prone, facing away from her with his arm dangled across her belly. When she pressed a kiss into the warm salty skin of his shoulder, his arm tightened as though he'd registered the affectionate gesture through his slumber. She contemplated this natural intuitive quality of Jase's. That sensitivity was what made him such an excellent newspaperman . . . and also what made their relationship so dangerous. As time passed, she wouldn't be able to hide her falseness; of that she was certain.

Being careful not to wake him, Reba lifted his arm and rose from the bed. The red gypsy skirt and striped pirate's shirt lay on the blue carpet where they'd been so hastily discarded the night before. She picked them up and draped them over a mahogany chair before walking over to the large multipaned window.

She stood gazing out at the mist-shrouded lake, unconcerned that Jase might wake and see her clothed only by pearly morning light. Her lack of modesty surprised her. Somehow this grand house and Jase's formal bedroom felt as comfortable as if she'd lived here forever.

And she knew why. It was because sometime during the night she's passed over the boundary into love. She was utterly, foolishly in love with Jase Kingsford.

She feared her heart would pay the consequences.

DURING THE FOLLOWING three weeks Jase seemed everpresent in her life; whenever he couldn't be with her, he kept her company in her thoughts. Her emotions seesawed from euphoria to despair, her heart and conscience at war. On several occasions Jase questioned her about her moodiness. Everyone seemed to be noticing it. This day it was Debbie who tried to break through Reba's reserve.

"I might be able to help if you'd just open up to me," Debbie said at the end of their shift when they entered the nurses' lounge. While changing into a metallic-green dress, she contemplated Reba. "We've talked before about the men in our lives. Why not this time? You'll feel better if you tell me what's wrong."

Reba sank down onto the imitation-leather couch and let her head fall back. She stared up at the plain white plaster ceiling as if its blandness could smooth out her thoughts. "I don't mean to shut you out. I appreciate your concern. I really do. It's just that . . ." She closed her eyes and rubbed them wearily. "It's so complicated. I have to sort things out for myself."

"Just remember my crying shoulder is available anytime. I even make house calls."

Reba straightened, opening her eyes again and watching bemusedly as Debbie clipped on a pair of huge faux-emerald earrings to complete her dinner outfit. Even when she'd begun dating her straitlaced doctor, Debbie had not attempted to hide the flamboyant part of her personality. She put on a false front for no one. It was a quality of her personality that Reba had always admired.

She wished she could be so open with Jase, but she knew he wouldn't understand. She'd promised herself she'd make a clean break from him once her month of riding with Becky was over, but now she was so in love with him that she wondered if she could keep to her decision.

Tired of her own problem, Reba focused on one of Debbie's. "So tonight you're going to meet your dearly beloved's dearly beloved parents," she said, seeking her friend's mirror-reflected gaze. "Nervous?"

"Are you kidding? My knees have been shaking all day. There's no getting around it, though. It's something I have to do." Despite Debbie's excited expression, doubt clouded her eyes. "It's his mom I'm really worried about. Mothers don't like me. Never do."

Reba thought it likely that conservative Bob's mother might not see past Debbie's flashy style to that wonderful person within.

"What I'm really dreading is telling his parents that I was married before," Debbie said. "I told Bob right off when we started dating. He didn't care, but his parents might think of me as secondhand goods."

"It doesn't matter what they think," Reba said.

"I know. I hope they like me, but that isn't crucial. It's what Bob feels that's important." She cracked a wry smile. "True love triumphs over all . . . even parents."

And lies, Reba added to herself, the truth of Debbie's words shining into her mind like a beacon of hope. Perhaps it was time to follow Debbie's example and tell Jase her secrets. If he loved her, he might understand and forgive her. But did he love her? She was certain of her own feelings; she could only guess at Jase's. Until she knew for sure he was in love with her she must keep silent . . . and yet she knew she must also speak up at some point. She would wait until Christmas, she decided. Surely, if he hadn't fallen in love with her by then, he never would.

"I'm just going to think of this as a challenge," Debbie was saying.

Her world suddenly brightened by a ray of hope, Reba smiled broadly. "That's just what I was thinking, too."

THE PUNGENT ODOR of seawater enveloped Reba as soon as Jase assisted her out of the Bronco. Spending Sunday afternoon at Seattle's downtown waterfront had been his idea. Earlier they had dropped Becky off at the stable to ride with her friends, and Reba was glad for the chance to spend a few hours alone with him. Something was on his mind; she'd sensed it since he'd picked her up.

They stood at Alaskan Way, waiting for the light to change. When it did, people surged around them in a rush for the three o'clock ferry to Vashon Island, one of the numerous islands dotting Puget Sound. Jase took Reba's hand as they crossed to the sidewalk that ran along the piers. She loved the way he continued to hold her near him as they strolled along, gazing like tourists at the shops and restaurants in the refurbished old pier buildings.

"How about this one?" He gestured toward an indoor-outdoor seafood stand where sea gulls cried for handouts.

"Great. I love the alder-smoked salmon," she said as she inhaled the scent of the fish and the briny sea air. They took their food to one of the wooden park benches that overlooked the choppy gray water of Elliot Bay. Reba put her nose close to her meal and took a deep breath again. "Mmm. This smells fabulous! I'm so hungry I think I'd steal crumbs from the birds."

"You and Becky both." Jase sat beside her, close enough that their thighs touched. "I suppose I ate all the time, too, when I was her age, but it still surprises me how suddenly ravenous she can be."

"And she never gains an ounce, I'll bet." Reba remembered how thin she had been as a teenager. Oh, for that metabolism again.

"I think she's beginning to." Jase began devouring his meal with a hearty appetite of his own.

Reba listened to the water's splash against the oily black pilings and to the chatter of the crowd surrounding them. The heavy overcast sky and unseasonable cold weather hadn't daunted the tourist trade.

"I've been trying to figure out how to handle something with Becky," Jase said suddenly.

"I thought something was bothering you."

"It is," he admitted. "You know, you think you've got everything resolved and then these old issues come up again." He flung the last of his salmon out over the water. A large grayish-white gull caught and swallowed it midair. "I thought Becky had accepted the idea of being adopted and felt secure about it. But last night when we were watching a special about the problem of teen pregnancies, she became moody. Apparently most girls keep their babies these days. Some schools even have nurseries. Good or bad, the trend now is to keep the child no matter what. It brought Becky's old insecurities to the surface again. She always had uncertain feelings about her natural parents. As much as she loved Carolyn and me, she still hated the thought that her birth parents didn't want her."

"Didn't want her?" The words burst out of Reba in hot fury. Not at Becky, but at life...at fate. She averted her face until she regained her composure. "How did she get that idea?"

"I don't know. It's not strange for her to wonder."

"It appears she's jumped to conclusions."

Jase shrugged, his handsome face lined and troubled. "Come on, let's go. You're shaking from the cold."

Reba was shaking, but it had nothing to do with the temperature. Inside of her repressed emotions fought to be released. She realized that she must not only tell Jase who she was, but also Becky. They headed at a brisk pace back to the Bronco.

"Is that what you believe, too?" she asked as he opened her door. "That Becky's parents didn't want her?"

Jase entered the truck and started the engine, switching the heater to high. "I like to *think* they wanted her," he said slowly. "What does it matter? I'm just grateful they made the decision to give up Becky. I can't imagine life without her."

"I know something about this subject," Reba pursued. "When I was sixteen, I had a friend who gave her baby up for adoption." She'd blurted out the admission before she could halt it, but on some deep level she felt glad. Perhaps it was a good thing to reveal a little of her past. If she explained the feelings of other pregnant teenagers she'd known, she might gain his sympathy when the time came to explain about herself. "Sharon's boyfriend took off, and her family refused any help," Reba said as they headed back to the stable. "What Becky doesn't understand is that times have changed. There used to be a lot of pressure put on girls to give up their babies. And most did, from what I understand. It broke Sharon's heart to give up hers, but everyone told her it was the best thing for her baby and finally she was convinced, too."

"It might help Becky if you'd tell that story to her. Of course she's been told a hundred times that her mother probably sacrificed her own feelings to give her child a chance for a better life. But hearing about a real situation might help her to understand."

Reba savored Jase's reaction to her tale. If only she could tell Jase the whole truth: Sharon had been one of the dozen girls staying at Birdie's home at the same time as Reba. All but one had chosen adoption. That Laney Sullivan had bucked the system and kept her child haunted Reba to this day, for it made her question her own decision. She glanced over at Jase's finely sculpted profile and wished she felt sure enough of his love to confide in him now. She thought about Christmas, only four weeks away. But, oh, the waiting was so hard.

The drive back to the stable might have given Reba her lesson in patience. The downtown streets were clogged with basketball fans heading for the Coliseum to watch the Sonics play. It began to rain, and by the time they reached the bridge over Lake Washington, the rain had turned to driving sleet.

The stable parking lot was nearly deserted when they finally arrived. So was the indoor arena. In the freezing rain Reba ran behind Jase to Amber's barn. The sounds of high-pitched squeals and laughter increased as they dashed toward the shelter of the barn roof. They arrived just in time to see Becky, dripping sponge in hand, chasing Heather down the center of the long aisle. Horses in stalls along both sides watched the commotion with bright dark eyes while they chewed their dinners. The few people in the barn paid little attention, more interested in finishing whatever they were doing and heading for the comfort of home. The girls raced to the far end and back again. Just as Becky came within striking distance, Heather, athletic and fast on her feet, dipped and dodged and dashed out of reach. Jase laughed at the girls' antics and slipped his hand around Reba's waist, squeezing.

"I'm going to miss this," he said. "It won't be long now till I lose this part of her."

"I don't know. I can't imagine Becky being one of those long-faced sullen teens. She's got too much fun in her." Reba added in a wistful tone, "you're so lucky you got to watch her grow up."

Jase drew her tighter to him. "You sound as though the parade has passed you by. You'll have children one day. I can't imagine your not being a mother."

"I know." Reba by now felt enough at ease with Jase to speak openly about some of her deepest feelings. "I've wanted to have a family for a long time now. It's been my dream, really."

Jase smiled down at her. "It's a nice dream."

A screech caught Reba's attention. Ten feet in front of them, Becky sprawled across a hay bale where she had evidently tripped and fallen. She lay with her cheek against the concrete, her booted feet kicking the air.

"I give up." She gasped as though she hadn't an ounce of energy left, and her feet fell lifelessly to the floor.

Reba noticed the sponge still gripped in her hand.

Heather, her head cocked suspiciously, crept closer to Becky in an exaggerated cat walk. She bent to peer into her friend's face, then screamed in delight when Becky sprang to her feet. Three of the nearest horses threw up their heads and snorted in alarm. Heather, her black hair flying out behind her and hazel eyes gleaming with excitement, dove behind Jase.

"Throw it out now. Throw it now, I dare you!" she challenged Becky.

"Cheat, cheat, cheat!" Becky cried indignantly, wobbling a little on her feet.

"All right, girls. The game's over," Jase ordered. "You're going to get wet enough running for the car." He reached behind him and pulled Heather forward gently. "Do you two have your horses groomed and your saddles put away?"

Heather nodded. "We just finished when Becky splashed water on me." She grinned at Becky and made a face. "I splashed her back, and she came after me."

Still staggering, Becky plopped down on a nearby tack trunk. Reba noted that Heather's eyes were bright from the fun and her cheeks a healthy rose pink. Becky, on the other hand, had gone from flushed to deathly pale. She leaned forward, her elbows on her knees, swaying a little. Reba studied her daughter with a nurse's eyes and a mother's worried heart. Becky rubbed her forehead with a grimy hand, leaving a muddy streak on her damp brow. Shooting a concerned glance at Jase, Reba went over to crouch at Becky's feet. She pushed back the thick blond hair to see an odd expression on Becky's face. "Are you all right, sweetheart?"

"I feel funny."

"How?" Reba felt for Becky's pulse. It was beating rapidly. She placed a hand on her forehead. Temperature normal. She looked into the blue eyes. They were unfocused.

Sweat trickled down Becky's cheeks. "I'm dizzy."

"Just sit here a minute, honey." Reba sat down beside her on the tack trunk and took her hand. It was trembling and wet with perspiration. Reba automatically logged Becky's symptoms and attempted to match them with an illness. Perhaps it was just the flu, but she didn't think so. She told herself there was nothing to get into a panic about. The best thing to do was get Becky home.

Just as Reba stood to beckon Jase, Becky muttered something unintelligible and toppled forward. Reba caught her and tried to pull her to her feet. Her daughter lay in her arms like an eighty-pound rag doll.

"Jase," Reba cried, struggling to keep the inert form from falling to the concrete. "Oh, God!"

Instantly Jase was there, lifting the limp weight from her. "I'm taking her to the hospital." He headed at a fast pace toward the truck, with Reba at his side holding Becky's hand, and Heather trotting behind. "Heather, we need you to make a phone call," he ordered, not harshly. "You know Dr. Estrada. He's your doctor, too, isn't he?"

When Heather nodded, he said, "Call his answering service. Tell him we're on the way to the Emergency Room at Eastside General Hospital with Becky. Then call home and have someone pick you up."

"Yes, Mr. Kingsford." Heather began to sob. "Is Becky all right?"

"The truck's unlocked, Heather," Jase said, looking down at Becky's closed eyes. "Open the passenger door." He glanced at Reba. "I'll hold Becky while you drive."

Reba didn't want to release the young hand she held, but she had no choice. She swallowed hard and took command of her emotions. When Jase had settled himself in the passenger seat with Becky nestled in his strong arms, Reba turned to Heather.

"Everything is going to be fine," she assured her in a soft voice. "I'll call you as soon as we learn something." Heather's eyes were still rounded in fear. Impulsively Reba pulled the child to her in a quick, compassionate hug, then scrambled into the driver's seat.

At the ER Reba was glad to find Debbie on duty. As Jase described Becky's symptoms to the medical receptionist, Debbie saw to it that Becky was placed on a gurney and wheeled into the first examining room. She took Becky's blood pressure, pulse and respiration while Reba and Jase watched in tense silence.

"I'm going to take a blood sample. I'll just prick your finger," Debbie warned the unconscious girl.

Reba placed her hand on Becky's shoulder. "It'll sting, but not for long." She wondered if Becky heard her at all.

Debbie was preparing the blood-sugar test when Dr. Estrada arrived. The gray-haired, middle-aged man shook hands briskly with Jase and then skimmed over the records.

He examined Becky and the result of the blood-sugar test while Jase and Reba observed, their hands clasped. Dr. Estrada ordered an intravenous injection of glucose solution.

Reba kept her eyes fixed on her daughter's face, and after a minute Becky's color returned.

Becky blinked and opened her eyes. "What's going on?" she asked, her gaze drawn to the tube taped to her wrist. "Oh!" she exclaimed.

"Thank God," Jase whispered and squeezed Reba's hand. He stepped forward so that Becky could see his face and spoke soothingly. "Everything's fine. You've just given us another exciting run to the hospital, but you're fine now." Only when he was certain his daughter no longer felt afraid did he turn to Dr. Estrada. "Could this be related to the concussion she had last month, Bill?"

"No, I don't think so." Dr. Estrada wrinkled his forehead, causing his heavy silver brows to meet. The doctor's years of experience and his kindly spirit showed in his gray eyes. "You didn't have another fall, did you, my young equestrian?"

Becky shook her head. Reba recounted the events in the barn and Becky's symptoms. The doctor nodded, eyes narrowing, and she guessed what he was thinking. He turned his attention to Becky again, who was looking normal. When asked, she assured him she'd been feeling fine, except for having headaches and feeling tired more often lately.

"And how's your appetite been?" Dr. Estrada asked.

"Good, I guess."

"Better than normal, maybe," Jase said.

Reba met Jase's eyes. They were both remembering that afternoon's conversation. "She can eat maybe two, three hamburgers in a row," Jase volunteered.

"How about today?" Dr. Estrada asked. "What did you eat?"

"I didn't. I overslept and there wasn't time."

"And last night for dinner?"

Becky gave her father a guilty look. "Heather and I were going to buy hot dogs before the movie, but we were in a hurry, so we just ate candy bars."

"Sounds like you're in a hurry too much of the time, young lady," Dr. Estrada chided. "Don't you eat Ingrid's cooking anymore?"

"I usually do. Can I sit up now?"

The doctor chuckled. "In a few minutes." He glanced at Jase and then addressed Becky in a casual tone calculated not to alarm. "I'm going to step down the hall for a few minutes with your dad and Miss McCallister. Nurse Simpson will keep you company."

"I sure will," Debbie said. "How about a glass of orange juice, Becky?"

As soon as they entered the empty waiting room and before Dr. Estrada had a chance to speak, Jase asked, "What is it, Bill?"

He gestured toward the couch and then sat down across from Jase and Reba. "I'm not sure of the cause yet, but Becky's blood-sugar level and other symptoms indicate organic hypoglycemia."

"Hypoglycemia? You mean low blood sugar?"

"Exactly. Contrary to popular notions, hypoglycemia is *not* a common clinical condition in the general population. But Becky does have the symptoms."

"Is it serious?" Jase asked.

"It could be, if untreated. Fortunately hypoglycemia is fixable. But first we have to figure out what's causing it. That's why I'd like to keep Becky here overnight and run some tests. We should have all the results within a week." He frowned. "As I recall, Becky's genetic history is not complete. Is there any way you could get more information on the birth parents?"

"The records are sealed." Jase's jaw jutted forward, and Reba went numb with fear as she heard his words. "But I'll do my damnedest to see what I can find out about them."

8

REBA SLAMMED AROUND her little house, scooping up her dirty clothes and towels and stuffing them into the washer. This was the first time all week that she'd come home early enough to do any household chores. She'd volunteered for extra shifts just to avoid Jase. Only when she'd felt reasonably sure he'd be out of the house did she call to check on Becky, who was doing fine. As long as he searched for the birth records, Reba didn't want to see him.

She let the lid of the washer drop with a clang and then wheeled the vacuum into the living room. Without giving Bushka any warning, Reba turned on the machine next to the pet bed where the huge yellow animal was dozing. Startled, the dog bounded for the bedroom with her tail between her legs.

Why did Jase have to be such a determined, do-it-now type of man? Reba wondered as she furiously shook out Bushka's bed and sucked up the long yellow hairs. There was no need yet for Becky's genetic history. Dr. Estrada had only cautiously advised that a need might arise, and she knew that possibility was remote. If the time came when Becky's family medical history was required, then she of course would help— even if it meant revealing herself as Becky's mother.

She kicked the dog's bed back into place. To have her secret exposed without good reason infuriated her.

Adoption records were supposed to be kept secret to protect all parties. It was the law. But rich, powerful men had influence; Jase had that on his side, plus sympathy. Everyone would want to help a man devoted to his child.

With the roaring whine of the vacuum cleaner, she couldn't quite be sure the phone was ringing. She turned off the switch. It was. She debated whether to answer because she knew it could be Jase, calling again to tell her he missed her and giving her a progress report on his parent hunt. Then all at once she was racing for the phone, fearful that he might give up before she reached it.

"Hello," she gasped, hoping to hear his voice in spite of her misgivings.

"Don't tell me you're at home," he said. "I thought you lived at Eastside General."

"They finally had enough of me. They said I needed a little sun. I was beginning to match my white uniform."

"I've got great news for you about Becky."

"Oh?" She held her breath in suspense.

"She's fine. All the results are in, and there are no complications and no special treatment other than a well-balanced, high-protein diet. Smaller, more frequent meals...the way she's been eating this week. Bill says that with that life-style she'll probably live longer and be healthier than most of us."

"That's wonderful." The words rushed out, and the tension she'd felt all week was gone. Now Jase could drop his parent search. "I told you I didn't think there was anything to worry about."

"So from now on I promise to listen to my personal medical advisor. How about dinner? It's been awhile." He added with quiet emphasis, "I've missed you."

His simple declaration sent waves of excitement through her. A few minutes ago she would have made an excuse, but now her world had turned around again. The crisis that prompted Jase's probe into Becky's background had passed, and once again she hungered to see him. "I missed you, too," she said. "Dinner sounds wonderful."

"I'll be there at six."

Jase arrived at a quarter to six, with roses and kisses. Once again he managed to throw her off balance.

"Extravagant, aren't we?" She took the dozen long-stemmed silvery-lavender roses from him, then eyed the tissue-wrapped bundle in her arms. No one had ever presented her with such a gift before.

"You deserve them. You're an exceptional human being."

"And an extravagant compliment to top it off. I'm terribly flattered." And she was.

Knowing his way about her small home quite well by now, Jase went to the correct cupboard, brought out a large crystal vase and filled it with water. Centering it on her oak dining table, he asked for the flowers and then tore off the green floral paper to place one rose in the vase.

"You're gentle," he said, then positioned another rose next to the first. "Gorgeous." Another rose. "Intelligent." Another. "Compassionate." He took the remaining eight roses in both hands and plopped them in with the rest. "And sexy—as hell."

Reba laughed in sheer delight, and Jase folded her into his arms. Simply being held by him made her feel as though explosions were going off inside her. "Sexy, hmm? *You* definitely have your share of that quality," she murmured.

He gave her a cocky grin. "I know."

She didn't have time to laugh again before he pressed his lips against her. Her mouth softened and opened of its own accord. They remained locked together until they were literally pushed apart. Bushka was wedging her huge shape between them.

"Bushka is jealous of your attentions," Reba said. Bushka had gone through three weeks of obedience school training by now and proceeded to sit as Reba commanded. Still, the dog whacked the floor with her tail and eyed Jase like a love-starved adolescent until he crouched to stroke her head. All training evaporating, Bushka bounded to her feet and lapped Jase across the face.

He grinned up at Reba, who watched in mortification. "I'm going to have to take a rose back," he declared. "You fail as an animal trainer."

"No one's perfect."

Jase stood, his eyes skimming her two-piece fuchsia dress. "Oh, you're close, my dear. Dangerously close."

Reba quirked a brow, reaching for her coat. "We'd better go eat."

As they drove across the bridge, the car phone beeped. It was Jase's answering service saying that Birdie Pennington had returned his call. It would be all right if he wished to see her this evening.

Reba listened to the message, stunned. Her thoughts were in such disarray she barely heard the operator giving Jase the address.

Jase replaced the receiver with a triumphant smile. "This is a real breakthrough. Birdie Pennington is the woman who runs the residential shelter where Becky's mother stayed. I can't wait to talk to her."

"We're going there now?" Reba asked, her heart racing.

"It's practically on our way. I hope you don't mind. It's great you can go with me."

Reba sank down into the leather seat, wishing she could simply disappear.

Jase, in his enthusiasm, didn't notice the trauma his words were causing Reba. "You know," he said, "your appeal from the medical point of view might give me a little leverage with this woman. Every link in the chain of Becky's adoption was kept completely secret. It really took some work to get the name of this shelter, The Sunshine Home, out of the adoption agency. The private adoption agencies in this state have historically made their own rules about adoptive records. Especially twelve years ago. It might be hard to get information out of The Sunshine Home, too."

"But there is no medical emergency anymore," she said, keeping the desperation she felt from her voice.

"That's true, but I'm not waiting until there is one. Who knows what life holds?"

What, indeed? thought Reba. She could just imagine Birdie's surprised look when Jase introduced her. And then, quite likely, Birdie's outburst of recognition.

Jase went on. "This situation has just pointed out the need to get complete family medical records for Becky. I'm going to follow through on this right now. I'm not waiting for the trail to get any colder."

He headed up to Capital Hill, an older district now trendy, located only minutes from downtown Seattle. He turned left onto Broadway, a street alive with all manner of night stalkers. Reba stared blankly at the street people and the yuppies. A theater showing a French film, a restaurant with a witty name, a shop with neon clothes flashed by her. Everything, including Jase's voice, seemed far away as she focused all her concentration on her problem. There had to be a way out of this dilemma. She pressed her fingers to her forehead. Think! she ordered herself.

"Are you feeling all right?" Jase's gentle voice brought her back with a start.

"No," she blurted out as she realized the best thing to do was to find an excuse to be taken home. Though Jase would think it odd, since she had been in glowing health minutes before, it was worth a try. "I have a headache suddenly. How silly. I don't know where it came from."

"I have it too hot in here." Jase turned off the heater and continued before Reba had a chance to say more. "I really don't know what kind of cooperation to expect from this Birdie Pennington."

"I suppose she'll have to follow through with her policy," Reba said, praying that Birdie would tell Jase nothing.

"You forget that I'm practiced in the art of persuasion. Birdie Pennington," he mused. "I have a feeling this Birdie is going to sing."

He laughed at his joke, obviously confident of the outcome of this venture. When he glanced at her, she produced a wan smile and rubbed her forehead again. By now the headache wasn't faked. Again she visualized the scene when Birdie opened the door. She slid a sidelong look at Jase's handsome profile and imagined how his features would freeze as Birdie revealed Reba's secret. There would be the interrogation, then his inevitable outburst of rage.

He stopped at a light. Reba remembered where Birdie's home was as though she'd stayed there only the day before. They were exactly five minutes away. Apprehension churned her stomach. She had to stall.

He pressed on the gas.

"Jase!" She practically shouted out his name. "I have to get out. Please pull over."

He halted the car so sharply that the engine went dead in the middle of the intersection. "What on earth!" He started the car again, swung left onto a side street and pulled over to a curbside opening posted for cabs only.

"I'm sorry. This headache is making me feel ill. I'm not going to be any good to you at Mrs. Pennington's like this." The corner building across from them contained a bar and grill that had seen better days. Reba nodded to it and spoke urgently. "Let's go in there for a minute. If I get some food, I'll feel better, I know it. ER was so busy today I didn't have a chance to eat." She cut her gush of words off at once, realizing her behavior was enough out of character to raise his suspicions. Calling up every ounce of her emergency-room training, she took control of herself. "Please, Jase. If you don't mind," she forced herself to say sweetly.

Puzzlement flashed across his face. "This is not the kind of restaurant I had in mind for a celebratory dinner. However, I wouldn't want to be accused of denying a starving woman a burger and fries."

Reba suppressed a sigh of relief. "I'll make it up to you." This time her smile was genuine.

"I'll find a place to park, then."

No matter the ragtag appearance of the place from the outside, the crowd inside spoke of its popularity. They grabbed a pub table just vacated, still littered with glasses and wet napkins, and considered themselves lucky. The human noise beat at Reba's ears, making it hard for her to think straight. She could demand to be taken home but knew that would seem bizarre to Jase. The only other solution was to somehow get hold of Birdie and do some fast explaining. Looking around, she spotted the phone sign that pointed down the rest room hallway. It was a chance.

"Excuse me. I'm just going to go wash my hands." She rose, a bit unsteadily. "Would you order me a hamburger and a Coke?"

Reba fought her way through the mob only to find the phone already claimed by a belligerent-looking young man wearing a black leather motorcycle jacket. At least she was out of Jase's sight. The man reclined against the wall as if he planned to talk for the next hour. Folding her arms across her chest, she shifted restlessly from foot to foot. He turned his back to her. She would simply have to wait while he continued to try to coerce some unfortunate female into coming down and tipping a few back with him.

His girlfriend apparently had other plans because when the man hung up it was with a loud expletive. Reba released her pent breath and stepped forward.

"Not so fast, sweetheart. I'm not done yet," he said, dropping a quarter into the phone.

Reba couldn't stand there and wait until he found a girl with enough bad taste to socialize with him. Turning on her heel, she aggressively elbowed her way back to Jase.

She sat eyeing the gigantic gourmet burger and large helping of fries piled on the plate before her and summed up the situation. It was imperative to contact Birdie. Keeping one eye glued on the hallway, she slowly began to eat. She just had to bide her time until Romeo got a date.

"Are you definitely having Thanksgiving with your father?" Jase asked.

"I have to work during the day, but I did plan to spend the evening with him." It was amazing how natural her voice sounded. "Will Becky be disappointed?"

"Not nearly as much as I am. Right afterward she's heading for Palm Springs, as planned, to stay for the rest of her school vacation with my parents. I thought it would be a great time for us to get away, too."

Reba paid him only half her attention. Finally she saw the youth saunter out. She dropped her hamburger onto the plate. She had to get to the phone before someone else commandeered it.

"There's a pretty good snow pack up at Crystal Mountain," Jase was saying. "I hear the skiing's not bad. If you can get a few days off, why don't we go up Friday and stay the weekend?"

"Oh, sure. I'd love it." Reba rose, formed a delighted smile for his suggestion and said, "Excuse me again, Jase."

Before he could question her, she departed. This time the phone was free. After a fast perusal of the yellow pages she inserted her quarter and punched out the number. She waited, tapping out an impatient rhythm with her short nails. One, two, three, four rings. Surely Birdie would be there in the office if she were expecting Jase. On the fifth ring a young girl answered.

Reba swallowed, suddenly choked up. So many memories flooded her mind. "May I speak to Birdie Pennington, please?"

"I'm sorry. Mrs. Pennington isn't here right now."

Reba opened and closed her mouth, not knowing how to proceed. "When do you expect her?"

"Oh, very soon. She's just gone on an errand." The girl sounded bright and happy, eager to please.

"I see."

Silence dangled between them until the girl spoke again. "Can I give her a message?" she asked cheerfully.

"Yes," Reba said. "Yes, of course. Listen carefully. Tell her that Reba McCallister is coming. Tell her to *please* pretend not to know me." Reba paused. "Do you have it?"

"Yes, I do. I wrote it down. Oh, this is exciting," the girl gushed.

Reba heard the sound of footsteps approaching behind her and looked over her shoulder to see Jase's concerned face. "Don't forget," she said into the receiver before ringing off. She turned to Jase. "Oh, I am sorry for jumping up like that. I just realized I'd forgotten to write down a medication on a patient's chart. He's supposed to get it at seven o'clock." The fabrication spilled out like water from a tap.

Back at their table, Jase sat studying her with concern darkening his eyes. "You seem so nervous. That's not like you. Is something wrong?"

"Sure. I'm tired, that's all. It's been a long day."

Jase didn't look as though he believed her, but he let it go. "Do you want to finish your hamburger, or shall we head out?"

They couldn't leave until Birdie had had time to return. "I hate to see good food go to waste." Reba picked up the remains of the hamburger, soggy and cold now, and fought down her nausea. She bit in and chewed with determination.

For a grueling twenty minutes she worked steadily at her meal. When Jase noticed she was nearly done, he flagged down a waiter for the check. "I hope you're feeling better now," he said. "Are you ready to go?"

She gave him a weak smile. "As ready as I'll ever be."

Jase drove them to a large turn-of-the-century brick house, one of many in the once elite neighborhood. Seeing the old place stirred up more painful memories, but she pushed them to the back of her mind so she could concentrate on her immediate problems. Her options were to stay in the car or go to the house. If she did the latter, fate lay in Birdie's hands.

Reba decided to take her chances with her old friend. Her body and mind numb with trepidation, she walked to the door with Jase. Someone answered the bell at once, and Reba stepped back, wishing she could hide behind Jase's broad shoulders. For a moment she wondered if the door had opened by itself, and then she lowered her line of vision. She had forgotten how short Birdie was, like a plump little quail hen. Her brown hair was now heavily flecked with gray, but it was still pulled up into the tight topknot Reba remembered. Her sharp black eyes darted from Jase to Reba, where they lingered a fraction too long.

Uncertain if the message had been relayed, Reba girded herself for the worst. All at once the small woman sprang into action, opening the door wide. "You must be Mr. Kingsford," she said.

Jase nodded and placed a hand on the small of Reba's back, pressing her forward. "This is Reba McCallister. I'm glad you can take the time to talk with us this evening."

To Reba's great relief, Birdie showed no reaction to hearing her name. Her attention seemed to be solely on Jase.

"Yes. Well, I knew how anxious you were for an appointment, and we have several girls due to deliver this week. I always go to the hospital with them, so I thought perhaps it would be best to see you before I became completely unavailable."

They entered a dark mahogany-paneled vestibule that opened to a spacious living room where a dozen girls lounged in front of a blaring television. The noise level rose when it was time for a contestant on a dating game to make her choice.

"My girls," Birdie said, chuckling with amusement as the girls shouted advice to the contestant. "We're like a family here."

A chubby blond teenager gave Reba a grin and a curious look. She must have been the one who took the message.

Birdie gestured toward the first room to the left, an alcove under the stairway. "Let's go into my office." She motioned for Jase to lead, and when he'd passed, she caught Reba's eye to give her a conspiratorial wink.

Birdie's office was more utilitarian than ever, Reba noted. Battered file cabinets, a large metal desk and several straight-backed chairs. Always short of funds, Birdie spent the money on her girls, not on decor.

When she sat, her desk dwarfed her. Jase positioned his chair close to Reba's, and Birdie's eyes moved from one to the other, not quite concealing her speculation about their relationship.

Jase leaned forward, clasping his hands. "As I explained on the phone earlier, I'm here about my daughter, whose mother stayed here more than twelve years ago."

"I will try to help you all I can, Mr. Kingsford."

"When Becky was an infant, my wife and I adopted her through our attorney, George Waterman. We knew then that it was the policy of the adoption agency not to reveal much of the parents' background. We were only given their ages and the general information that they were healthy. We accepted that at the time because we had no choice and also because we didn't really think it mattered." He paused, and Reba thought how his straightforward, unrushed manner added weight to his words. "I've learned differently. This past week I was confronted with the possibility that Becky's medical records might be absolutely essential. The present emergency seems to have passed, but I want to be prepared if the need ever does arise." He nodded toward Reba. "Miss McCallister here is a nurse. She's aware of the need for genetic records." He waited for Reba's corroboration.

She cleared her throat and met Birdie's confused eyes. "You don't need to reveal the parents' identities. Just medical information."

"I'd like to learn all I can," Jase said, contradicting her. "To tell you the truth, at this point I would like to know who her parents are."

"I don't know...." Birdie looked flustered. Although the room was cool, Reba felt perspiration trickle down her spine.

Jase pursued his argument. "There is a new attitude toward opening birth records, as I'm sure you're aware. Advances in medical science have changed the picture." He rose and thrust his hands into the front pockets of his gray wool trousers. "Organ-transplant patients, for example, have their best hope with blood-related donors."

Birdie rallied. "I am a nurse, too. So I am certainly familiar with medical advances, Mr. Kingsford. I will tell you straight off that I will not break my vow of confidentiality. In most cases the parents are guaranteed that the records will be forever sealed. They have been promised that this birth will remain a secret from their neighbors, relatives, future spouses and children." She slid a pointed glance at Reba as she uttered her final words. "I have been entrusted with the confidence of many young people. I will always try to honor that."

Jase bent, placing his hands flat on Birdie's desk. His expression held leashed anger and frustration. "Surely for the sake of a child you can bend your rules."

A lesser soul might have broken under Jase's assault. Birdie's black eyes flashed back at him. "It may not be possible to have what you want, Mr. Kingsford. I remember Becky's background. After you called, I went through your daughter's records. Her mother had listed no genetic illnesses. We don't have any information on Becky's male parent. That's often how it is."

"In that case, the mother should be appealed to for his identity. Then she could be interviewed."

A silence fell upon the three of them as they each regrouped. Reba's glance fell on a stack of brochures lying on the desktop. A photo showed a pensive young woman, and the cover read, Are You Pregnant, Confused and Not Sure Where to Turn? The teenager might have been Reba. Fifteen years old and so alone.

Birdie opened a desk drawer and handed Jase a form. "Fill this out and I'll see what I can do," she said, not unkindly.

When they returned to the car, Reba fell, emotionally exhausted, into the seat. It was hard to believe she'd come out of the experience unscathed. She offered Birdie a silent thank-you for not exposing her. She'd been given a reprieve. For how long, she didn't know.

Jase placed his hand on her cheek, brushing her hair back in a tender gesture. "You were a big help to me in there."

"No. I hardly said a thing."

"*I* certainly did." His face showed his displeasure at the way he'd conducted himself. "I'm just glad you were there to keep me from making a complete ass of myself. I wanted to rip those file cabinets open with my bare hands while you sat there cool and collected, reminding me to be reasonable." He exhaled audibly.

"When it comes to people I love, I go overboard. I'm afraid I lost my professional cool."

"Pressing for the parents' identity could have been the wrong track," Reba suggested, taking advantage of his respect for her rationality. "You might have better luck when you speak to Mrs. Pennington again if you concentrate on genetic information."

He turned over the engine with a vicious twist of the key. She knew his anger was not directed at her, and that his determination was as great as ever. He muttered, "If she doesn't cooperate, there are other recourses."

"The records are sealed."

"I'd be willing to go to court to have them unsealed."

Just when she'd begun to hope, defeat slammed her down.

The tougher the going was, the harder Jase would fight. If he had to, she knew he would track down the father himself. Reba knew he would not give up until he had what he wanted.

9

SNOW FELL like soft, silent feathers, tickling Reba's nose as she rang the doorbell at the old brick home. Under one arm was an oblong box, and tucked safely in her purse was a letter for Birdie to give to Jase.

She yawned, tired from being up most of the night. It had been impossible to sleep until she decided her next move. If Jase demanded more information about Becky's mother and father, she knew she must find a way to give it to him. She hoped that the letter in her purse would appease him for a while. She'd included everything about her own family except their identities and had promised to contact Becky's father.

Keeping that promise might be difficult. As far as she knew, Steven had left Seattle years ago, and she had no idea where he had gone.

At the sound of someone coming, Reba lowered her gaze in anticipation of Birdie's appearance. But when the door opened, she had to raise her focus, for it was not short Birdie who opened the door. A tall young girl stood looking down at her and smiling. An oversize gray sweatshirt with a decal of Mickey Mouse covered her swollen midsection.

"Oh, it's snowing!" Swept away by the infrequent event, the girl stared past Reba to the sugar-sprinkled yard and trees. "How perfect for Thanksgiving tomorrow." Remembering her manners, she grinned apologetically at Reba. "I'm sorry. Can I help you?"

"I'm Reba McCallister. I'd like to see Birdie." Reba pulled off her red knit cap and shook the wetness from it. Although she hadn't called in advance, she knew Birdie would be there. The girls would need her more than ever during the holidays. "Is she busy?"

"I'll say. We're making a huge meal, and everyone's helping in the kitchen." She laughed, cradling her belly. "Birdie is trying to organize us, but it's hopeless. Come on in. I'll get her."

After the girl had disappeared, Reba advanced to the living-room doorway and looked around. Ancient but comfortable-looking sofas and overstuffed chairs had been arranged in a conversation grouping. On the far wall stood the old upright piano on which Birdie had played while Reba and the other girls gathered around and sang. Near six-foot-high arched windows stood card tables, an unfinished Monopoly game on one, a Trivial Pursuit game on the other. Scattered across a coffee table were well-thumbed issues of *Seventeen* and *Cosmopolitan*. A history book and doodled notebook lay abandoned on the floor, along with soda cans and fingernail polish and sneakers. More than twelve years and it all looked the same.

Only her emotions were different.

"Reba."

She turned, startled out of her reverie by Birdie's cheerful voice. "I was just thinking that nothing seems to have changed," Reba said.

"You have, my dear." Reba scrutinized her, clucking like a mother hen. "You've grown into a beauty. And you're a nurse now, too. I couldn't be more proud."

She opened her arms, and Reba stepped unselfconsciously into them. The years fell away; inside she felt sixteen again.

"Last night wasn't exactly the ideal way to meet again after all these years," Reba said.

Birdie dismissed the apology with a flutter of her hand. "I didn't mind. It was so wonderful seeing you again. I hadn't forgotten you, you know."

Two girls came thundering down the stairs and dashed past them into the living room. Birdie shook her head and laughed. "Let's go into my apartment so we can have some peace and quiet while we chat."

"Here." Reba gave Birdie the package. "It's for you and the girls." Birdie drew the lid off the silver roses and exclaimed. After stuffing her cap in a pocket, Reba hung her coat on the hall tree. "They're secondhand, but I didn't think you'd mind. I'm going on a skiing trip, and I didn't want the flowers to go to waste."

They'd just entered Birdie's private domain, a large sunny room near the kitchen, when the girl who'd come to the door arrived with a tea tray. Birdie sent her off with the roses.

"Will your young man be upset that you gave away his present?" Birdie asked Reba when they had settled in facing wing chairs.

One glance at the knowing expression in the older woman's eyes told Reba who Birdie suspected the gift-giver to be. "Not when I tell him where they are."

Birdie poured Earl Grey into a bone china cup and handed it to Reba. Poignant memories surfaced of the last time Birdie had invited Reba in for a private conversation. They had talked of Reba's future: her return home, her thoughts of becoming a nurse, her giving up

Becky. She'd been helped by Birdie's sympathetic heart and clear head, Reba recalled. And she had returned, Reba realized, not only to deliver a letter, but also to seek guidance once again.

Birdie settled back and sipped her tea as though she had all the time in the world. "I've wondered about you often," she said as she studied Reba with loving eyes. "You were one of my favorites, you know."

Reba flushed with pleasure. "I missed you, too. I thought about coming back to see you." She looked away, to the French doors and snowy patio beyond. "No. To be honest, I didn't want to come back. I did miss you—very much. It was just that it hurt too much, giving up Becky. I wanted to block that whole part of my life out of my mind."

"It was a surprise to see you last night." Birdie smiled, reaching over to pat Reba's knee in a motherly way.

"Oh, I'm so glad you aren't angry. I had no idea Jase was planning on seeing you. I was trapped."

"Jase, is it?"

Reba set her cup on the little mahogany coffee table and sighed. "Maybe I should start from the beginning." One of the burdens of secret-keeping was the loneliness it caused; it was a tremendous relief to at last have someone to confide in. As Reba began to talk, Birdie listened with an air of intense concentration. She didn't judge others; she only tried to help them with their problems. By the time Reba had explained hers, Birdie was nodding as though she'd already arrived at an answer.

"Well, what do you think?" Reba asked.

"There's only one thing for you to do." Birdie knitted her fingers together in a determined fashion and placed them on her wide lap. "You must tell him the truth as soon as you can."

"I'm terrified that he'll hate me."

Birdie considered that, frowning. "Now why do you think he would react so harshly?"

"Because of his stupid principles!" Reba pressed her knuckles to her head. "He has his newspaper's logo, Truth Above All, printed on his brain. I just know when I tell him he's going to condemn me. And maybe I deserve that."

"No," Birdie returned forcefully. "You deserve to be loved. If Jase Kingsford has a sympathetic drop of blood in his heart, he's got to understand you acted in a prudent manner. You couldn't have known things would happen the way they did. What's more, he had a great deal to do with your falling in love with him."

Reba wanted to be convinced. "He'll suspect my motives. He'll think I just want to be with Becky."

"If he can't see how much you love him, he's one foolish man."

"Jase and I are just beginning to know each other. I know I'll have a better chance of winning him over if I hold off my confession for a while. I just need to get him off my trail."

Lines of worry appeared on Birdie's brow for the first time. "Mr. Kingsford is a determined man. He'll get the information he wants—not from me—but he'll find a way. You'd better be honest with him before he learns the truth on his own. It would be impossible for him to understand and to forgive that way."

Reba's fingers were trembling as she unsnapped her leather purse and drew out the thick legal-size envelope. Inside were five typed pages. "I stayed up half the night writing this letter. It's anonymous...from Becky's mother. In the letter I've explained that you contacted me. I've given all the medical information about my relatives that I know, and I've promised to locate Becky's father." Reba drew in a long breath and handed it over. "I included a couple of pages just for Becky, too. It's about the circumstances of her birth and how bad I felt about having to give her up. I hope Jase will let her read it."

"Do you know where Becky's father is, then?"

"I have no idea. There's no phone number for either him or his parents—or any Hjortlands with published numbers in this area. But I'm not about to give up." She rose to go, giving Birdie a hug that left her laughing and gasping. "I just pray I'll find him before Jase does."

IT DIDN'T FEEL like Thanksgiving, Jase thought.

The turkey tasted great. Becky was enjoying herself. All was well in his world . . . or should have been. The trouble lay somewhere deep within. It was an empty feeling that all the turkey and dressing and cranberries in America couldn't begin to fill.

He pushed aside the TV tray he'd been using, unable to face another bite of the delicious meal Ingrid had prepared. Beside him Becky consumed the foods she was allowed while one of the Disney movies they'd rented played on the VCR. Maybe he should have insisted on dinner at the table. Maybe that would have made it seem more like a holiday.

But probably not. Jase knew damn well what was making him so nervous and edgy. Reba wasn't here.

If he could just talk to her, he knew he'd feel better. Picking up the portable phone from the table beside his recliner, he punched out her number. After six rings he muttered an oath under his breath and was about to hang up when he heard Reba's gasping voice.

"Hi! Hold on while I catch my breath."

"Did you just get off work?" he asked, suddenly not content with the mere sound of her voice but yearning to be with her.

"Yes. I just walked in the door. Hold on a minute, will you?" Muffled sounds came across the line, then Reba was on again. "I had to put groceries in the kitchen. Working half the day and then trying to make a holiday dinner is probably not the smartest idea I ever had. I'd like to just order a pizza and relax. Dad is expecting me now, though."

"What about this weekend? Can you get off?"

"It's all set. I was able to trade for working on Christmas."

Disappointment flared. He'd been hoping to spend that holiday with Reba, too. "Your schedule is horrendous. I wish I could do something about it."

"You and me both."

Jase knew that she must be anxious to get busy with dinner, but the sound of her voice acted like an addictive drug. He kept her on the line by saying how well Becky was doing and explaining her new diet regimen. Reba, in turn, told him the details of her day at the hospital. When Jase spoke again, his voice had lowered to a more personal pitch. "It's only five now. How long will you be with your father?"

"A couple of hours, I guess."

"Why don't you drop over here afterward?"

"You're hard to resist, but I don't think I'll make very good company," she answered regretfully.

At her refusal his yearning for her grew more intense. It had been this way since the beginning: the more she resisted, the more he desired her. "I don't expect you to come and entertain us." Jase knew he was pressuring her, but he couldn't seem to help himself. "Becky and I are just planning on a lazy evening. We've got some good movies. Why don't you join us?"

"It sounds like fun. I really wish I could come." She paused, and he could sense her searching for words. "The truth is, seeing Dad can be a strain. I don't know what kind of shape I'll be in when I get home."

"You two still don't get along?" It wasn't always easy to keep peace with his own dogmatic father, but he felt it was his duty to make the effort.

"I told you before what my dad is like." Her tone was abrupt. "We had a falling out when I was a teenager. Over the years he hasn't tried very hard to patch things up between us."

"Come over later and we'll talk about it," Jase said.

"I'm beginning to view persistence as a very undesirable quality."

"How do you feel about stubbornness?" he accused, frustrated at not getting his way.

The sound of a long indrawn breath whistled across the line. "I'm going to hang up now," she said.

"Reba. Don't. I'm sorry." Jase noticed Becky had turned her attention from the television to him. At her amused expression he narrowed his eyes in mock fury at his daughter. He lowered his voice. "Reba, listen. I don't know what happened between you two, but I'm sure your father was doing the best he could at the time. If you have trouble understanding your father, get him to talk about his childhood. You might be a little more compassionate if you learn what made him the way he is."

"Good advice, Mr. Kingsford." Her sarcasm canceled her praise.

"More good advice. Why don't you make up with him? Why don't you ask for *his* forgiveness?"

"Honestly, Jase—"

"And that's another thing. Try honesty. Tell him how you really feel."

"I'm late. Goodbye, Jase."

The sound of the dial tone whined in his ear. *Good going, Kingsford. Good going.*

REBA COULDN'T GET her conversation with Jase out of her thoughts. Long after she'd hung up, it continued to circle like an endless tape in her mind. She considered it while she emptied her refrigerator of the Thanksgiving groceries, dropping the food heedlessly into the grocery bags at her feet. What pained her most were the doubts Jase had stirred in her breast. She'd always felt such indignation at the shabby treatment she'd received from her father. He'd been the one who'd wronged her; he'd made her suffer.

But he'd suffered, too. Reba stared at the celery stalk in her hands as she contemplated that. How devastated he'd been by her pregnancy. She remembered how he'd cried—actually *cried*—in front of her mother's photograph, begging forgiveness for his failure. Their daughter had gone bad, and he had blamed himself.

Reba finished packing the food and set the bags on the counter as she got her coat. She had been wrong to rebel in such a foolhardy way, Reba admitted to herself. Of course, she truly had been in love with Steven, but that didn't excuse her actions. She'd known about the facts of life; she'd known about birth control. The truth was, she'd been a thoughtless and pigheaded twit.

It was time to air the laundry, Reba decided as she drove to the house where she'd been raised. Long past time.

Reba arrived at her father's, primed from her mental pep talk. She juggled the two overflowing bags and stabbed at the doorbell.

"You brought too much food," he barked in greeting, his square frame blocking the doorway.

Flinching from his criticism, Reba nevertheless produced a sunny smile. "What's Thanksgiving without a lot of leftovers? This way we'll both have enough food so we won't have to cook all next week."

Gus McCallister was a man's man. Hard as bricks inside and out, he seldom showed a tender emotion and was uncomfortable with women. He believed in what he called "good, old-fashioned values," the kind that had been instilled in him early and firmly. He'd taken pride in living up to these values and had tried to implant them into his children. Perhaps his greatest fault had been in demanding that Tom and Reba conform to his rigid expectations.

Reba couldn't help noticing how silver his once thick curly brown hair had become. Old age was coming fast. She felt a tug at her heart. No matter how uncompromising her father was, he loved her deeply. Of that she'd never had a doubt.

He reached for both bags, giving her no choice but to relinquish them. Looking more at ease with a chore to complete, he took a moment to inspect his daughter as she took off her coat. "I want you to take anything left over home. You're too skinny."

"It's nice to see you, too," she said sweetly.

"Humph."

She followed him into the kitchen, still with its worn 1950s linoleum and faded blue gingham curtains. As her father took the groceries from the bags, Reba reached for her mother's tattered cookbook. "I already cooked the turkey in the microwave at my place. I've got all our favorite things: candied yams, pumpkin pie, oyster dressing, mashed potatoes. I wish Tom and Beth and the kids could be here," she said, thinking of her brother in California. "Remember when they came up last summer for the Fourth of July, and Tom incinerated the barbecue grill?" She rattled on, talking about holiday meals of the past when she truly wanted to discuss Becky and Jase. She and her father had never been able to share personal matters. To make it worse, ever since the day she had packed her things and taken her shameful pregnancy out of his house, there had been a wall of ice between them.

"I've been thinking a lot about how much fun holidays used to be when Mom was alive," she said, searching for a way to break that ice.

"I wish you'd turned out more like your mother."

Reba gritted her teeth against the sting of his words. "It must have been hard having a daughter like me."

"You were always too damn independent for your own good."

Reba turned her back to him and began to scrub the tar out of a potato. Her father said nothing more, returning to the living room to watch a game just as though she wasn't in the house. Bitterly she wondered why she'd bothered to try at all.

At least the day wouldn't be wasted, Reba consoled herself. While she was here, she could search her room for a clue to Steven's whereabouts.

She managed to get through dinner and back into the kitchen to do the washing up without uttering a single sharp word to her father, although at times he tempted her. She was filling the mashed potato pan with hot soapy water to soak when the phone rang. Then her father was at the kitchen doorway.

"A fellow named Kingsford's calling for you."

"What?" She stared at him stupidly for a split second. Drying her hands, she reached for the kitchen wall phone and turned her back to her father, signaling for privacy. He continued to stand there, just as he used to do when she'd talked to Steven.

"Hi." Jase's voice stroked like velvet. "I wanted to tell you I spoke out of turn earlier. You should have insisted I mind my own business."

"Consider yourself told."

Deep, masculine laughter rumbled through the wire. "Okay, I will. How's it going?"

"How did you get this number?" Reba asked, avoiding his question. "It's unlisted."

"Sources."

"Ever heard of the right to privacy?" Reba glanced over her shoulder and was surprised to find her father gone. "Never mind. I'm glad you called. My spirits need lifting—badly."

"I'm sorry to hear that."

Reba heard the underlying condemnation and bristled. After all, Jase didn't know her father or their situation. "I've tried talking things out with him," she said tightly. "He doesn't make it easy."

"Try one more time," he urged. "Do it for me."

"Don't you ever give up?"

"Just think how wonderful it would be for you two to make amends. It's worth pushing for, believe me."

"All right," she agreed reluctantly. "One more try."

"I'll pick you up early tomorrow."

Reba hung up and, needing time to think things over, took the back stairs up to her old bedroom. She liked visiting the large corner room. Everything was just as she'd left it—faded yellow spread on a single bed, complete Black Stallion series in the low case beneath the dormer window, battered window desk. Although she'd occasionally taken something she needed out of the room, it hadn't really been disturbed over the years. She walked over to the desk. The surface was dusted. It was the first time she'd realized that her father kept the room clean. It astounded, then touched her. She concentrated on pawing through the mess in the desk drawer, finding high-school papers, old magazines, letters, but nothing from Steven. He'd never written her. Shoving everything back into the desk, she slammed the drawer shut. Steven had told her his folks had come from out of state, that he had no relatives in the Northwest. He'd introduced her to a couple of his friends, but she couldn't even remember their names. A sound startled her, and she swung around to see her father walking in with two cups of coffee.

"How thoughtful," she said.

"You didn't make any," he answered, his voice gruff. Instead of leaving, he sat on the edge of her bed and stared out the dark window. He looked up at her where she stood, leaning warily against her old maple desk. "I heard you up here making all kinds of noise," he said.

"I'm sorry if I disturbed you," she said coolly.

"Nah, you didn't. I just came up to see what you were doing."

She heard the loneliness in his voice and scolded herself for answering him so frostily. Her ingrained resentment made her cruel. It seemed doubtful that she and her father could ever change their old ways of reacting to each other, but in her mind she could almost hear Jase urging her to try.

"I was just going through some of my old papers," she said, crossing the room and perching on the other end of the bed. "This was a nice room for me. There was plenty of space for my things here. I guess you didn't have your own room when you were a boy."

"I sure didn't. Us four boys shared a room."

"I suppose things were a lot different then."

He snorted. "I'll say. In those times parents made the rules, and the kids didn't dare argue. I tried to raise you and Tom to have that respect, too."

"Oh, Dad. Having opinions and wanting some control over your life isn't being disrespectful." Reba was wondering how to proceed when Jase's suggestion flashed into her thoughts. *Try honesty.* She knew she must confront the past if she intended to resolve anything. "There's something we should talk about," she said, speaking quickly before she lost her courage. "Have you ever wondered what it was like for me when I left here? When I was pregnant?"

His eyes widened. "I've thought about it. You never brought it up."

"I am now. I think you should know." Her fingers clamped viselike around her coffee mug. "It was very hard for me. I wanted to keep the baby, you know. She was something of my very own." She didn't hide the bitterness in her voice. "But it wasn't possible. I knew I couldn't support her. I wanted so much to be independent and take care of my child." She looked into his eyes, dark like her own. "You taught me that—to be independent and proud."

He frowned and spoke painfully, as if he were dragging the words from his heart. "I guess you got that from me, all right. The independent streak. The false pride."

She studied him, his muscular arms in short sleeves folded across his chest so that she could see the scrollwork of his Death Before Dishonor tattoo. His features seemed firmly set again, but his chin wasn't as square as she remembered it. The edges had been softened by time.

"There's no changing the past," he said. "I might want to do it, but there's no way I can."

She knew that was as much of an apology as she would probably ever get from him.

"I'm sorry, too, Dad," she said. "I'm sorry I wasn't the kind of daughter you wanted." She thrust out her chin in determination. "Dad, I . . ." The words stuck in her throat. She swallowed and started again. "Dad, I want you to forgive me for becoming pregnant. And for being so angry with you all this time. I hurt inside and I blamed you for it."

There, she'd said it. Amazingly, a sense of well-being came over her.

"That's all over and done with," he said.

"Not anymore." She looked into his remorseful eyes. "I've found Becky again."

He opened his mouth, then closed it again, at a loss for words. When his shocked expression faded, wonder filled his face. "Where? How?"

"It was a miracle," she said, overcome by his display of feeling. She had never thought he cared what had happened to Becky. Suddenly Reba found herself eager to tell him the whole story. She began with her accidental discovery of Becky and ended with the reason for searching her desk. How easily it had come out! And there her father sat, nodding in a most understanding fashion. "So, you see," Reba finished, "I've already decided I will explain everything to Jase, and also to Becky. But not just yet. I don't think he's ready to hear it."

The silver-haired man sat absorbing all he'd heard. As Reba waited for his response, she felt like a teenager all over again, wondering if he was going to disapprove of her actions.

He rose to his feet. Reba followed suit.

"This is the damnedest situation I ever heard of," he began, and Reba's heart sank. "But under the circumstances, I think you're doing the right thing. In fact, I'm proud of you. You've taken the side of the right, and you're fighting for it."

Reba stood as frozen as the snow outside. Then, before she realized what she was doing, she crossed to her father. He took an awkward step closer but didn't hesitate to open his arms to receive her.

"Oh, Daddy, thank you so much," she murmured, hugging him close.

Embarrassed, he pulled away. "Here, young woman. Get hold of yourself. I want to tell you something." His tone caught her full attention. "That Hjortland boy. I know where he might be. He came by once when you were still at that there girls' home. Said he was heading up to Alaska to fish with his uncle and you could reach him there. I told him you'd decided to put the baby up for adoption. He seemed relieved."

"You never mentioned any of this before."

"He was heading out. I thought it would upset you."

Reba heard the worry in his voice. He was brave, she thought. Just when they'd begun to build a new relationship, he'd risked bringing it crumbling down. What was more, she believed that at the time he had truly done what he considered best for her. He'd been looking out for her.

"You might call Dutch Harbor information," he suggested. "Maybe he's still up there."

"You don't know how much this means to me," Reba said.

"I think I do." He cleared his throat. "I'd like to see her, ah, Becky. You don't happen to have a picture?"

Reba smiled, so full of joy she could barely contain herself. "As soon as I can, I'll bring one over. She looks just like Mom."

When they returned downstairs, Reba served pumpkin pie, and they ended up talking for two more hours. Their problems hadn't all been solved that night, but they had begun to build a better relationship, one that Reba intended to cultivate with great care.

It had been an amazing day.

10

WHEN THE PHONE RANG at eight o'clock that evening, Jase immediately thought it would be Reba calling to say she'd changed her mind and wanted to spend the rest of Thanksgiving Day with him and Becky. But at the sound of Birdie Pennington's voice his heart began to pound in anticipation of an entirely different sort.

"I have good news," she was saying. "A letter's been delivered here for you . . . from Becky's mother."

"Who is she?" he demanded.

"As I'm sure you must understand, she doesn't want her identity revealed."

Jase suppressed the frustration that had caused him to snap at the helpful woman on the phone when he should have been thanking her. He'd got action, faster than he'd hoped he would, and for that he was grateful. "I appreciate your efforts, Mrs. Pennington. I'll be right over."

Jase returned home an hour later to find Becky in the den where he'd left her, putting the last rented movie into the VCR. He stood in the doorway for a long moment, watching his daughter and wondering what effect this new information would have upon her. The letter he'd read while at Mrs. Pennington's not only contained the medical answers he'd requested, but also a long personal note to Becky. In it the woman gave a detailed account of the circumstances surrounding

Becky's birth and told of her fight to keep her child. It was obvious from the emotional tone of the writing that she loved Becky very much and had regretted giving her up. Would it help Becky to know that her real mother cared so much? Jase wondered. Or would Becky be tormented by the fact that she had a loving mother out there somewhere who was unable to be with her?

"Becky." The tension in his voice caught her attention, and she glanced questioningly over her shoulder at him. "Turn off the TV. I have something to show you."

"An early Christmas present?" she teased, following him over to his easy chair and sinking down to sit cross-legged at his feet.

Jase handed her the thick envelope, contents intact. When she looked into his sober eyes, her brows rose in question. "What's this?" she asked, turning the fat envelope over in her hands.

"Since you've been diagnosed as having hypoglycemia," Jase began, "I've been trying to locate your natural parents to learn their medical histories. Not that I'm worried about anything," he hastened to add, "but just as a precaution. I found out that your natural mother stayed at a home for unwed teenage mothers, and I went there to ask the woman who runs the place for any help she could give me. She contacted your mother."

Becky stared up at him, her mouth opening and closing, but no words emerging.

"That envelope contains a letter to you from her." Jase nodded toward her frozen hands.

"My real mother?" she forced out in a whispery voice. "Oh, Dad." She gripped the envelope, then quickly recovered. "When am I going to meet her?"

Jase shook his head, angry at himself for allowing Becky to think that might happen. "I'm afraid she wants to remain unidentified."

Becky continued to look straight at him while she absorbed that disappointment. Then with trembling fingers she unfolded the papers, taking her time to read each page thoroughly before turning to the next. Jase waited in silence until she had finished. "Now you know how your real mother truly feels about you. You don't have to worry about that anymore." He reached down to smooth the wavy blond hair back off her taut face.

Suddenly Becky burst into action, leaping to her feet and flinging the letter into the air. Her cheeks had turned a fiery red, and she bit down on quivering lips. "I hate her! I wish I'd never read that stupid letter!"

With pages still floating down to the carpet, Becky fled the room.

Jase tore after her as she stormed up the stairs, but he forced himself to come to a halt at the slammed door of her room After giving her several minutes to calm down, he gently twisted the knob and pushed the door open. Perching on the bed near her, he placed a comforting hand on her shoulder. "It's all right to feel confused," he told her when at last she sat up. "Hearing from your mother after all this time. It's come as quite a surprise to you."

"I didn't mean what I said—you know, about hating her. I just . . ." She shrugged, unable to straighten her tangled thoughts into sentences.

"I think you're probably glad to know she loved you and didn't want to let you go."

"Why doesn't she want to see me?"

"I couldn't say. She probably doesn't want to disrupt the life you're leading now with me." Jase didn't say what he guessed might be the truth—that she was embarrassed by her pregnancy and wanted that part of her past to remain a secret. He wondered what he would have done if the woman had asked to see Becky, and his stomach knotted at the mere contemplation of it. Thank God he didn't have that to deal with.

Becky gazed up at him, the fury leaving her face. "That's it," she said with certainty. "She must know that I have the greatest family on earth. She doesn't want to butt in and maybe mess things up for me."

Jase pulled his daughter into his arms for a fierce hug, squeezing until she began to laugh at his exuberance. "You're absolutely right, sugar," he said heartily. "She loves you, and she's thinking about your best interests." Jase let her fall from his arms and bounce on the bed. After giving her hair an affectionate ruffling for good measure, he rose to go. They'd talked enough; now she needed time to think this through for herself. She was already over the shock of it. He was certain that soon she would feel relieved and at peace with herself. Many of the questions she'd struggled with for so long had been answered, thanks to the thoughtfulness of her unknown mother.

For that, Jase would be forever grateful.

THE NEXT MORNING Jase arrived at Reba's door at nine o'clock sharp. The weather was as happy as his mood, the sky cloudless and the air refreshing with that invigorating quality that late autumn brings. He rolled back on his heels, feeling about as self-satisfied as a man could get.

He couldn't wait to see Reba's expression when he told her about the letter. He didn't like the way he'd pressured that poor old woman at The Sunshine Home, but his tactics had worked. That letter had come like a wondrous present from out of the blue, bringing enormous relief.

Now he could put Becky out of his mind and focus totally on Reba, which was what he looked forward to doing during their long three-day weekend. The thought of having her all to himself sent a jolt of anticipation through him. It seemed as if they never had enough time to be alone together. No. That wasn't true. They spent a great deal of time with each other. It was just that he wanted more. He wanted her night and day, day after day. She lived in his mind, and a longing for her constantly ate at his gut. He'd experienced these symptoms with a woman only once before, and never this fiercely. Good Lord, he had it bad.

The sound of the chain being released caused his blood to surge. Reba let him in, clutching her maroon velvet bathrobe below her breasts.

As soon as he had stepped in from the cold, Bushka jumped up and Max also appeared out of nowhere, the way cats seem to do, to wind himself about Jase's legs. Reba's large brown eyes drew him to her.

"Move off," she scolded the animals in a sleep-husky voice. "I want this guy all to myself." She burrowed her arms inside his unzipped jacket and hugged him close, sending a surge through his veins that made him want to forget skiing and carry her right back to bed.

"You have no competition, believe me," Jase said before cupping her face and capturing her mouth, kissing her urgently enough to express the strength of his feelings. She arched her body against his so that her belly pressed against his arousal. "To hell with early starts," he muttered and swung her easily into his arms.

Her robe fell open to expose her breasts, enticing him further. Reba laughed softly up at him, cheeks rosy with desire. "Do I have any say in this?"

"Yes. And you've said it."

"I don't recall—"

"You didn't have to speak." He carried her to the bed, lowering her slender form to the rumpled blankets. "Your body has a voice of its own."

She gazed in the direction of his groin, a mischievous light in her eyes. "So does yours." Her fingers worked at his belt buckle. "Let's give them something to talk about, shall we?"

An hour later Reba insisted that Jase shower alone. "I don't want you getting ideas," she said, eyes bright and face flushed with a just-made-love-to glow. "My bags are packed. I'm eager to get going." When he finished with the bathroom, she took it over. "Why don't you make yourself useful in the kitchen? I desperately need a cup of coffee."

Reba, dressed in jeans and a navy turtleneck sweater, arrived in the kitchen by the time the coffee was ready. She placed her packed suitcase with the skis, poles and boots piled next to the front door and came to sit beside him at the kitchen counter.

The round in bed had left him feeling relaxed and content. The excitement of being with her remained, mellowing now to a more comfortable sensation. "Did the roses wilt already?" Jase asked, noticing the flowers were gone from the round oak table. He didn't recall seeing them in her bedroom, either.

Reba busied herself pouring the coffee into her mugs with the sea gulls on them. "I took them over to Mrs. Pennington's place for the girls. Since I was going to be gone, I thought someone should be able to enjoy them. I hope you don't mind." She handed him a cup, and Jase thought her expression seemed guarded.

"When did you go there?"

"Before I went over to Dad's." She bent into the refrigerator, emerging with a package of English muffins, butter and strawberry jam. Smiling over her shoulder, she asked whether he wanted one or two.

Watching as she placed the muffins in the toaster oven, he noticed tension in her efficient movements despite her outward cheer. "So you had dinner with your father and lived to tell the tale," Jase explored. She put a plate of muffins in front of him. How dark her eyes looked. Her curly hair, combed now, shone like mink. "Did you try honesty?" he asked.

Her discomfort appeared to vanish as quickly as it had arisen. She brought her cup of steaming black coffee to her lips and blew ripples across the surface. "It went well—no, it was fantastic. He opened up. I never thought we could be friends again."

"Is everything cleared up?"

"It'll take a while, I think. But we made a breakthrough last night. I'm never going to let us go back to the way we were before."

Jase marveled at Reba's strength. It was never abrasive but as gentle and feminine as every other aspect of her. He saw the fire in her spirit every time he peered into her eyes. He could look at those brown eyes for a hundred years, he thought as she gazed back at him with her soft mouth curved into a pleased smile.

"It was mostly your doing," she said. "Before you called last night, I had been ready to leave. I *couldn't wait* to leave. Dad and I were miserable together, just like always."

"Old patterns." He waited for her to go on, enjoying her triumph.

"We've begun to sort out our differences—thanks to you. I wouldn't have swallowed my tender pride and made the first overtures if you hadn't kept harping at me."

Jase drew back, his own pride smarting from her light slap. "Harping? Is that what I do?"

"Let me phrase it this way: sometimes you don't know when to quit."

"An admirable quality, one which has proven its worth many times." Jase grinned, thinking of the letter. "Most recently with Birdie Pennington."

"What do you mean?"

"Mrs. Pennington contacted Becky's mother. The woman immediately wrote a long letter and hand-delivered it to Birdie. She called me right away, and I went over to pick it up." Jase ran a hand through his hair, still astounded by the sudden turn of events. He'd been prepared for a long, hard battle. "It was an incredible letter, Reba. Not only did she outline her family's medical history, she included a letter to Becky. It was as though the woman knew how much Becky needed reassuring. I'll tell you, I've come to hold great respect for Becky's mother."

"So you let Becky read it?" she asked in a breathy voice, her eyes even darker and brighter than before.

Jase remembered Becky's stunned face when she read the letter and the sound of her crying into her pillow late that night. Not since her adoptive mother's death had she let herself go like that. It was as though all the pain she'd held inside had come rushing out like water over a dam, and she'd finally been rid of it. The letter proved her natural mother had wanted her, and still loved her even to this day.

"Becky was overcome," he said softly. "It was a catharsis for her."

"You look relieved, too."

Jase nodded. "The woman said she'd locate Becky's father and get information from him, also. Her response was so prompt and thorough that I'm confident she'll come through."

Reba rose and went to rinse their cups in the sink. "So you're not going to keep searching for the man?"

"At this point I don't think I need to."

"It's all turned out so well," Reba said, sounding as relieved as he was.

"So far," Jase qualified, coming up behind her and turning her to face him. "Let's forget about all that and just enjoy ourselves this weekend. I know I've been obsessed with this issue, and it's probably been a strain on you, too. We won't talk about Becky all weekend. I want this to be a special time for us."

Reba couldn't agree, but she didn't say as much to Jase. This weekend, when she had his undivided attention, would be the ideal time to tell him the truth. Jase hadn't yet told her he loved her, but that didn't matter. She knew he was in love. She could see it in his eyes, hear it in his voice, sense it in his touch. She'd been waiting until she had no more doubt; now that time had arrived.

She gazed into the blueness of his eyes and said with feeling, "This weekend will be one we'll remember for a long, long while."

THREE HOURS LATER they were seven thousand feet above sea level, in a world totally different from the city they'd left behind. Dark olive-green fir trees contrasted with the white snowy peaks that surrounded them. The chair lift brought them to the end of their upward journey, and Reba skied off the ramp onto Quicksilver Run. Determined to have fun despite her anxiety over the upcoming confrontation, she tried to put her decision out of her mind.

The terrible foreboding faded as Jase drew up beside her, his mouth curved into an infectious grin. He looked as though he'd stepped out of a ski magazine in his sleek royal-blue jumpsuit with his sandy hair dancing in the breeze.

"I love it up here," he said. "There's something about being in the mountains that touches your soul."

"I feel it, too," Reba agreed. "The grandeur has a way of humbling you—putting your puny problems in perspective."

Overhead the sapphire sky was almost too brilliant to look at. Looking around in wonder at the glittering sunlit snow, Reba knew how Crystal Mountain got its name. Before them descended the easy slope she'd chosen, the broad expanse of packed snow alive with weaving colorful skiers.

A group of four young boys sailed past them, letting out whoops of joy as they attacked the slope. Next an elderly couple began a more sedate descent. All the people at the resort—no matter what age or race or sex—had one thing in common: the love of starting high and going down fast. The thrill of mastery and sense of flight gave skiers a special euphoria. Reba cocked her head toward Jase, sorry her inexperience kept him from the fun of the steeper runs. "This isn't quite heli-skiing down vertical virgin snowfields," she commiserated with him. "I wish I were better at this."

"Don't worry." He winked at her. "By spring I'll have you flying down Exterminator like you'd been born on skis."

She put on her goggles and zipped her white jacket, preparing to start out. She'd been skiing with boyfriends before, but never had she felt so electrified. Jase motioned for her to lead, and Reba planted her poles in the snow to push off. For a few minutes she focused all her concentration on getting started down the hill. As her confidence grew, she looked around and found him skiing parallel to her. The sight of his lean body swaying in expert lazy curves down the mountain awed her, his expertise making her feel awkward. Finding her own rhythm at last, her turns began to smooth into a line of graceful Ss. Every once in a while Jase would catch her eye and flash her an encouraging smile. By the time they skidded to a stop at the bottom, she felt as though effervescent wine were pumping through her veins.

"I'd forgotten how much fun this is," Reba said as they skied to the lift line. "I could do this all winter."

"It's a date." Jase's eyes sparked on hers, warming her all over.

They took the slope twice more before locking their skis on the metal rack near the lift and heading off to find a place to eat lunch. In no hurry, they strolled among the crowd. At first the sheer number of people was daunting, but soon they discovered themselves caught up in the holiday mood all around them. Overhead the midday sun blazed down upon them with vigor, but the snow on the ground had not begun to melt and it crackled merrily beneath their feet as they went along. The sprawling complex consisted of alpine lodging, shops and restaurants, all nestled in the frosty white bosom of the Cascade mountains. After browsing through the ski shop, they headed inside the main building. The first restaurant they entered was a huge informal café where metal picnic-style tables were arranged end-to-end. A swarming mass of humanity packed the area. Jase and Reba looked around, both noticing at the same moment the marathon lines of people waiting to order hamburgers or chili dogs.

"How about going upstairs to the pub?" Jase suggested, frowning at the disheartening sight. "You look like you could use a warm-up drink, anyway."

"You must have read my mind."

Taking her by the arm—a gesture intended more to keep from losing her in the throng than of affection— he led her into the bar. The situation there turned out to be similar to the one below. Every table had already been claimed. Others who didn't have a place to sit milled about the bar drinking in friendly groups, their ski boots causing them to walk in a funny stiff-legged fashion. Reba spotted a couple leaving a table nearby.

Grabbing Jase's arm, she began pulling him in that direction. They rushed for the empty chairs and sank into them, laughing delightedly at their stroke of luck.

Jase leaned over to give her a quick peck on the cheek, his dazzling smile thrilling her to her toes. "You're a marvel," he said. "How did you manage to snag us this table before the rest of this madhouse got to it?"

"I don't know what came over me," she said in all honesty. "It's amazing where a little determination will get you." They were still chuckling when the waiter arrived to take their orders for Irish coffees and sandwiches. All the while Jase held her hand beneath the table, and she reveled in the feel of his strong fingers twined with hers. The exercise, the cold fresh air, the beauty of the landscape and the company of the man she loved all combined to make her feel on top of the world.

"I needed this time alone with you," Jase said after the waiter departed. "With everything that's been happening, between us and with Becky, it seems as though most of the time I go around in a sort of daze. I'm either thinking about you or worried about her. It's even affecting my work." His mouth quirked into a self-deprecating grin. "Last week I was so irritable I fired my best reporter three times."

"Apparently he knew better than to take you seriously."

"*She* was getting pretty annoyed with me. The last time I fired her, I had to bribe her back to work with a raise and this weekend off."

The waiter returned with their drinks, and Reba took a sip of the scalding liquid, enjoying the combination of sweet whipped cream, rich coffee and potent Irish whiskey. "That's not as bad as me," she admitted. "Last Wednesday I bandaged a man's ankle."

"What's wrong with that?"

"It was his wrist that was sprained."

They laughed their way through another Irish coffee each and their roast beef sandwiches. By the time they'd finished, it was a struggle to get back to the slopes. One more round of drinks and Reba knew they would have been too intoxicated with alcohol and each other to do anything but end up back at their hotel room in bed.

But the cold fresh air was invigorating, and by the time they'd reached the top of the run, both were eager to ski the afternoon away. A group of youngsters, making wagers on who would reach the bottom first, charged past Reba and Jase. The kids' high spirits were contagious. Reba cast a challenging sidelong glance at Jase.

"Race?" She began pulling out ahead.

Jase hooted in disbelief, halting to zip his jacket. "Are you kidding?"

Picking up speed, Reba was a good three yards ahead when she yelled back over her shoulder, "See you at the bottom, slowpoke!" With all the energy she could muster, she took off down the hill.

Jase watched her go, surprised and amused by her antics. Of course she had no chance of winning the game; he was a far better skier than she. But maybe he would let her think she'd won. Starting after her, he took care to stay a fair distance behind, following her as she moved away from the crowded middle to ski the less populated tree-lined edges of the run. He discovered that he liked staying behind her. In this position he had the advantage of observing her all the way down. And she was indeed an exquisite sight with her slender body curving in a sensual back-and-forth pattern and her dark hair bouncing on the shoulders of her white ski suit. He'd never thought of skiing as a sexy sport, but Reba certainly gave it that quality. He noticed the snug fit of her suit against her bottom and thighs. . . .

"Jase!"

Jerked out of his revelry, Jase flashed an annoyed glance at the woman who skied up beside him. "Anne." His anger vanished when he saw the grinning face of one of his reporters. "I see you're making good use of the time off I gave you," he shouted.

"Yep." She laughed, skiing in perfect sync with him, her long blond hair flowing out behind her. "I'm making good use of the extra money, too. So any time you want to fire me again, just go right ahead."

Anne had lost track of her husband, so she and Jase continued to ski together while she tried to locate him. Anne, with her infectious good humor, was one of his favorite employees. She always had a funny story to liven up his day whenever he happened to see her at work, and now she had him laughing at her description of her husband learning to ski. Jase finally spotted the big bearded man weaving awkwardly not far off, and Anne departed to catch up to him. But when Jase looked around to find Reba, she was nowhere to be seen.

REBA FOUND HERSELF among the trees and suddenly realized she'd gone off course. She'd looked back to make sure Jase was behind her and had been surprised to see an attractive blonde skiing beside him. She must have stared for too long, for now she was deep within a shadowy forest of snow-draped firs. Jase must be wondering where she'd gone.

Or was he? The last time she'd glanced back, he was laughing out loud at something the woman was telling him.

Reba puzzled over who she was. Someone he'd dated? Or recently met? One thing was certain—he found her entertaining.

Reba skied more slowly now, her mind still on Jase and the fact that she really knew very little about his relationships with other women.

Maneuvering around the trees, which were becoming denser, she decided she'd gone far enough. She slid to a halt and sank the tips of her poles deep into the soft, pristine snow. Though she wasn't more than two hundred yards from the busy ski slope, the scenery had altered dramatically. Sunlight filtered through thick, drooping boughs to create a patchwork on the uneven snow, and the air smelled deliciously of resin. The dark green firs spiraled up a hundred feet to pierce the azure sky.

She had just turned around to start back when she heard the swishing sound of skis crossing snow. "Jase?" she called out, hoping the approaching skier would be him. When she spotted the vivid blue of his jumpsuit, her heart began beating rapidly. Suddenly he burst into complete view, heading toward her with reckless speed. His expression was a mixture of panic and fury.

That was when she felt her right leg slide downward into a rut, and she lost her balance, toppling sideways into a deep snowdrift. Knowing he'd be there in a second to help her, she sat up and matter-of-factly began unfastening her skis.

Jase came to a stop beside her. "Thank God I found you! Are you all right?"

"Nothing bruised but my pride." Ashamed to have caused him such worry, she averted her face and brushed snow from her sleeve. "I accidentally skied off course. Pretty silly of me."

He planted his ski poles near hers. "I'm sorry I didn't watch you more closely. I thought you could handle the run."

"It wasn't your fault," she assured him.

He quickly kicked off his own skis and sank down on his knees beside her, reaching for her shoulders to turn her around to him. "One minute you were right in front of me. The next it was as though you'd disappeared from the face of the earth. What happened?"

"I looked around when you were skiing with that blonde . . . and I guess I just wasn't paying attention to where I was going." She watched for the effect of her casual statement.

"The blonde?" He sat back on his haunches, considering her with narrowed eyes while removing his ski gloves. Tossing the gloves aside, he reached out to her and tangled his fingers in her thick hair. He leaned forward and tilted her head back to place a warm, tender kiss on the tip of her cold nose. Her snowy lashes fluttered downward, hiding her eyes.

"I have no interest in blondes," he told her fervently. "It's a brunette who has my undivided attention. One incredible brown-haired, brown-eyed woman. Do you have any idea who that woman might be?"

"Me?" Reba whispered, slowly raising her gaze to his.

"Give the lady a prize." He lowered his mouth to hers, hovering a fraction of an inch away for an agonizing moment before meeting her lips with his. If any doubts remained, his ardent kiss banished them. She was the one he wanted. When he withdrew his mouth, she could only gaze up at him in silent wonder.

"You have to know I've fallen in love with you," he said quietly. "It's been so obvious. I never expected to fall in love. But the truth is, you've had me from the very beginning. You've filled a void in my life. You're almost too good to be true. It's taken me awhile to believe the incredible luck of finding you."

In her joy at hearing his words of love, she suppressed her fear of how he would react when he learned that it was not luck that had brought her into his life. "Oh, Jase, you don't know how much I've wanted to hear this. I love you, too. So much that it hurts. I'm not the jealous type—but when I saw you skiing with that woman . . ." She shrugged and managed a grin.

"That was Anne Wells, the reporter I told you about. She's here with her husband."

Reba groaned loudly. "I really feel like a dope."

"How could I think of anyone else when I can barely keep my hands off you?" Turning his words into action, he tumbled her backward into the snow to pin her pliant form beneath him. The hard strength of his body sent thrills coursing through her. He hovered above her, his sandy hair falling forward and his feverish gaze locked on hers.

"Still jealous?" he asked.

"I never was—not really."

"I do love you, sweet Reba."

"You love me," Reba whispered, feeling as though her heart was about to burst with happiness. "Say it again, Jase. Tell me you want me as much as I want you."

"With words . . . or like this?"

He communicated his feelings by capturing her mouth with his, his kiss deepening almost at once to an intensity that had her reeling with ecstasy. His love-making had been incredible before; now that they'd shared their hearts, he seemed on fire with passion. She, too, burned hotter than ever before. She'd never known she could desire a man as much as this. Crazy with longing to feel his naked body against hers, to con-summate their love, she searched blindly for the zipper to his suit.

Jase's hand caught hers, and he released her mouth with a raggedly inhaled breath. "It's time we headed back to the lodge," he murmured, his voice gruff with passion.

Reba stared up at him, misty-eyed with emotion. "Oh, I don't know. I've never made love on a ski slope before. This might be an interesting experience."

"It might be a very chilling experience."

She thought about that. "Maybe you're right. But I'm willing to go only on one condition."

"What's that?"

She reached for the collar of his jacket and, grasping the material with both hands, pulled him down to her mouth for a last lingering kiss. "That we pick up ex-actly where we left off."

"That's a promise, definitely."

JASE PROVED HIMSELF a man of his word as he drew her nude body to his an hour later in the privacy of their darkened room. Reba found the chill of the outdoors still caught in his hair as she speared her fingers through its thickness, but the heat of a furnace was in his kiss. As he passionately caressed her lips, she twined her legs with his, luxuriating in the feel of his muscular calves and thighs. The slopes were fun, but the excitement of skiing couldn't compare to the thrill of being in bed with Jase.

In unspoken agreement they kept the pace of their lovemaking slow in contrast to the frenetic activity of the resort outside. He nuzzled her forehead and nose and neck, his lips continuing their downward exploration until they reached her breasts. He kissed circles all around her straining nipples, and when his mouth reached a taut bud, she uttered a little cry of delight. Wanting to give him equal pleasure, she slid her hand down the crisp hair on his chest to the smooth hardness of his arousal.

"Reba, oh, honey," he rasped, his control beginning to crack. "I'll show you just how much I need you."

The intense desire she'd experienced on the cold snowy mountainside reignited with his whispered passion. As he spread her legs with his, she inhaled sharply in expectation, but he surprised her by prolonging the delicious yearning with a deep kiss. As he probed with his tongue, every cell of her body seemed to tremble in anticipation of their union. Finally their bodies joined, and Reba cried out her love for him.

Later Reba curled contentedly in Jase's sleeping embrace. Too excited to drift off herself, she lay still in his arms and replayed the enchanted day over and over in her mind. Jase loved her. He'd said the words. But he'd said something else, too. She was too good to be true.

His statement reminded her of his devotion to honesty in relationships, and she could well imagine his horror when she revealed the facts.

She had no doubt that he loved her passionately. But his trust in her was new and fragile. Though she hated keeping this secret from him, she wished she could wait until his confidence in her grew stronger. At least, she rationalized, she would face all her past before she faced Jase with the truth.

She hadn't reached Steven yet. Perhaps tomorrow she could try again, if she had the opportunity.

How wonderful it would be to have all this subterfuge behind her. Deliberately she cast out her worried thoughts and tried to focus on what Christmas would be like with Jase and Becky.

In his sleep Jase tightened his arms about her. Suddenly she felt secure. She relaxed, turned toward him and wrapped her leg over the warmth of his flat male hip.

Tenderly she kissed Jase's sleeping face and then drifted off into blissful Christmas dreams.

"ARE YOU SURE you don't mind?" Jase asked the next afternoon as he slung his skis over his shoulder.

"Are you kidding? All I want now is to soak these aching muscles," Reba said as she massaged her calves. Their day had begun with lovemaking, followed by a full morning of skiing. Her exhaustion and Jase's eagerness to hit the expert runs were perfect excuses for her to remain behind. She yawned broadly and waved him off. "Go. Have fun. I'll be here when you get back."

After Jase had shut the door behind him, Reba forced herself to wait until she felt certain he wouldn't return. Then she leaped off the bed, tiredness forgotten as she rummaged through her purse in search of her phone credit card. While she had privacy, she would try again to reach Steven.

She had faced so much of her past. Finding Becky. Seeing Birdie. Talking honestly with her father. Each challenge she knew had been a necessary step.

Now she must deal with this last step: contacting Steven. With that done, she would be able to face the future and tell Jase everything.

Reba stared down at the slip of paper on which she had written the number the Dutch Harbor operator had given her. No one had answered when she'd tried calling before. Now her stomach contracted from nervous anticipation as she listened to the ringing phone. Again no answer. Fighting down her disappointment, she waited for fifteen minutes and then dialed once more. Another half hour and she tried again. Two hours later she'd just dialed for the tenth time when she heard the sound of a key being inserted in the door. She put down the receiver and lay on the bed, feigning sleep.

On Sunday, their last day at the resort, Reba made a final attempt. She'd let the phone ring for several minutes and was about to hang up when a man's voice answered.

"Hello," Reba said.

"Speak up," the man shouted over the background noise. Reba could hear what sounded like cheering and suspected a football party was in progress.

"This is an old friend of Steven Hjortland," Reba said loudly and distinctly. "Could I speak to him?"

"Steven Hjortland? Never heard of 'im."

Reba's heart sank. Had she been dialing the wrong number all this time?

"Let me have that phone," yelled a younger man in the background. She heard someone else calling for a beer and then a scathing remark about a touchdown that had just occurred.

"Oh, wait a minute," the first man told her. "I guess there's a crazy guy here who wants to talk to you, lady."

"Hello?" the younger man shouted. "Is this call for me?"

Reba swallowed the lump in her throat. "Steven? Is this Steven Hjortland from Seattle?"

"Who is this?" he demanded.

"Steven, this is Reba. Reba McCallister."

There was a long stunned silence. "Reba," he said in a quieter tone. "Where are you?"

"In Seattle. I know it's a shock to hear from me like this, but something important has come up that I need to discuss with you. Can you talk?"

"What's this about?" he asked warily. "I'm married now."

"It's about our child. Our daughter."

There was another pause as that sank in. His tone was gruff when he spoke again. "This is a bad time. The only other phone is in the kitchen where my wife is cooking dinner. Let me have your number, and I'll try to get back to you when I have some privacy."

Unable to predict the times she might be alone, she couldn't let him phone her at the hotel. "No. That won't work."

"Listen. Can this wait until next week? I'm coming down to Seattle on Friday. Can we meet somewhere?"

"Yes. Yes, of course. I'm a nurse at Eastside General. I get off duty at five. How about if we get together in the hospital cafeteria?" She hesitated before speaking again. "It's good to hear your voice, Steven."

"I'll see you on Friday."

Reba stood at the window, staring out at the white mountains as she pondered her next move. The weekend had been so beautiful up till now. Just thinking of telling Jase filled her with a desperate sort of dread. The promise she'd made herself became harder and harder to fulfill as the weekend wound to a close.

Expecting Jase back at any minute, she began to dress for the buffet dinner in the resort's restaurant where a skiwear fashion show was planned. After dinner they'd stay to hear the folk singers. It wasn't an atmosphere conducive to heartfelt confessions, Reba thought gloomily. Yes, perhaps it would be best if she waited until after she'd met with Steven.

THE ACTIVITY in the emergency room kept Reba running all day. She had just placed a bandage on the forehead of the latest in a stream of Friday rush-hour casualties when she saw Debbie coming on duty to relieve her.

"I don't envy your working tonight," Reba said as they walked to the station, its counter adorned with a huge red Christmas bow and miniature decorated pine tree. "It's been crazy in here all day."

"All week," Debbie amended. "Too many party goers out on the roads. 'Tis the season." She gave Reba a concerned look. "I hope you're not driving home in this mess."

"Nope. I'm going to have a nice leisurely cup of coffee and something to eat in the cafeteria first."

As Debbie ran to assist the medics who were wheeling in another traffic victim, Reba gathered up her things. It had been a hectic five days, but secretly she'd been glad of the diversion. Whenever she'd had a minute of inactivity, anxiety had overtaken her to make her life miserable. Today had been the worst because she knew she'd be seeing Steven.

She'd be glad to have this meeting over with. Until she'd put this business with Steven behind her, it would be hard to feel good around Jase. And Jase was a hard man to ignore. Since their return from skiing four days ago, he'd called twice, once to invite her to Becky's school Christmas pageant, and then to watch *Miracle on 34th Street* on TV. Finally she'd turned on her answering machine and stopped returning his calls. Every time she so much as spoke to him, she feared he would sense her apprehension. She was getting tired of answering his questions with lies; all she wanted now was for this matter to be finished. First, she would talk to Steven, then tomorrow, Jase.

Whatever happened, it would be a comfort knowing she had done all she could and a relief to place the final move in Jase's hands.

At the cafeteria entrance Reba scanned the half-filled room and spotted Steven easily. Not because he looked the same, for he didn't. The green parka he wore had Dutch Harbor, Alaska, imprinted on the back. He sat at a table in the center of the room sipping coffee, the lanky body she remembered replaced by the muscular physique of a man who was used to hard physical labor. When Reba approached, his gray eyes fastened on her, recognizing her immediately.

As he rose, she held out her hand, feeling awkward and uncertain. "Thanks for coming," she said, smiling.

He motioned for her to sit across from him, and they took a moment to assess each other. Steven's light brown hair was short now, and the face that had once been so beguilingly boyish showed the effects of his rugged life-style. Lines crept out from kind eyes, and a small scar marred his powerful angular jaw. Reba had wondered if she would feel any emotion toward him after all these years, but she wasn't surprised when none surfaced. Theirs had been a fleeting teenage romance.

"You said there was something about the baby," he began. His coarse hands, resting on the table, were clinched almost into fists. "I thought she was adopted right after she was born."

"She was. Don't worry. Everything is all right. The past isn't returning to haunt you," she said in an effort to put him at ease.

Relief passed over his face. "I'm glad you called, really. All these years I'd wanted to tell you what a stupid kid I was runnin' off like that. I wanted to tell you how sorry—"

"No. Stop it," Reba broke in. "I didn't look you up for some late-date apology. If you wouldn't mind, I'd like to put our mistakes behind us. I don't blame you for anything, Steven."

He regarded her intently. "I'm not proud of what happened."

Reba dismissed that with a shrug. "I bet I really caught you by surprise when I phoned."

"You threw me for a loop, all right." His wide grin relieved the tension between them. "I never told my wife, Pam, about the baby. When you called, I was worried she'd find out. Then I got to thinking about it and decided to tell her everything before I came down here. She's a good woman. There shouldn't be secrets between us."

"How did she take it?"

He gave a rueful snort. "She was more jealous of me seeing you again than she was upset about the kid. After all, that was a long time ago, before she knew me."

For a few minutes they shared details of their lives. Steven explained that he'd just purchased his own purse seiner and was making a good living in the commercial fishing business. Reba congratulated him, sincerely pleased that he was doing so well. Becky would be proud of him, Reba mused. Taking out her wallet, Reba handed him a photograph. "This is your daughter, Becky."

He studied the picture for a long time. "She don't look anything like me."

"She took after my mother," Reba explained. "That's how I happened to find her. Her photograph was in the gossip section of a local paper; when I saw it, I just knew it was her. She even has a brown spot in her eye, just like my mom did. Her adoptive parents kept her given name, as I had requested. Sometimes I still can't believe what a lucky accident it was my locating her again."

"Who adopted her?" he asked.

Reba hesitated, then decided it wouldn't be fair not to tell him. "The Kingsfords. You know, the newspaper people."

He let out a low whistle. "The kid's got it made."

Reba debated telling Steven the whole story of her deception. But there was no point in it; not as there had been with Birdie and her father. "She does have a good life. But not just because of the money and social standing. Her father loves her." Reba continued to tell him all she knew about Becky, concluding with her latest trip to the hospital. "Becky has hypoglycemia, a blood-sugar disorder. That's not fatal or anything, but Mr. Kingsford still thinks it would be a good idea to know her complete family history. You can never tell when that might be important. It's possible that it could save her life someday. I gave Mr. Kingsford mine already and promised to get hold of you." She reached into her purse again and placed a form on the table. "If you could just fill this out, it would be a great help." She indicated the self-sticking note she'd attached. "My address. You can mail it to me, if you'd like."

His brow creased in concern. "She's not sick now, is she?"

"She's fine. The hypoglycemia is controlled with diet."

Steven was glancing over the papers when Reba sensed someone's approach and looked over her shoulder. *Jase.* She couldn't hide her shock. He exchanged curious looks with Steven before turning his attention to her.

"Debbie told me I might find you in the cafeteria," he said.

She rose abruptly. "What are you doing here?" she asked ungraciously, her heart pounding like a sledgehammer.

"I've been worried about you." Jase cast a sideways glance at Steven before returning his assessing eyes to her. "You haven't been returning my calls."

"Nothing's wrong," she blurted out. She saw his gaze sweep across the table, his eyes widening when he saw Becky's picture lying there next to the medical history form. He bent slightly, scanning the paper.

Steven rose slowly to his feet. Noticing Jase's odd expression, he sent a puzzled glance to Reba. Things were spinning out of her control. She watched in frozen horror as Steven offered his hand to Jase.

"Steven Hjortland, old friend of Reba's."

Jase returned the handshake. "Jase Kingsford."

"Hey, man, it's good to meet you." Steven grinned, pumping Jase's arm. "Reba's just told me about you. I'm Becky's father."

11

JASE'S HAND FELL AWAY from Steven's, his intense blue gaze on Reba. "What's this all about?" he asked her with deathly calm.

Reba gripped the back of her chair to steady herself, her knees as trembly as soft pudding. As stunned as she was, some part of her mind continued to function with an odd clarity. Steven's untimely declaration destroyed her carefully made plans, but perhaps she could still explain everything to Jase. First she must get rid of Steven before he said anything more. Pulling herself together, she addressed Steven. "Would you mind leaving us? You can mail those papers to me, or call me later at home if you want to talk more. Okay?"

The tension in the air could have stopped a runaway horse in its tracks. Steven's gaze jumped from Reba to Jase, and he drew his big frame into a defensive posture. "What's going on here?" he asked her.

"That's just what I'd like to know," Jase said. "How did you find this man?" he questioned Reba. "And what's he doing here with you?"

"I asked him to meet with me."

"I think you've got a lot of explaining to do."

"Yeah," Steven agreed. "Something's stinking here."

Reba turned swiftly to Steven. "Please just go," she commanded, her authoritative tone undermined by a tremor of stress. "I'll call later."

Steven leaned toward her as if to shield her from Jase. "I'm not heading out until I know you're all right."

This unexpected solicitude punched at her self-control, and her hands began to shake. "Please, Steven. This is a personal matter between Jase and me."

"You're sure?"

"Yes. Yes. Just go."

He remained poised like an uncertain grizzly bear for a moment and then slowly reached for the papers. His large hand hovered above the photograph of Becky. "Can I keep this?"

She felt relief when he shoved the picture into the pocket of his parka and walked out of the cafeteria followed by the curious stares of the doctors at the next table. "We need to go somewhere private," she said, looking up into Jase's unreadable expression. She started for the door, only to be halted by his hard grip on her arm.

"You'd better tell me right now," he said.

"Not here."

"I won't be put off, Reba."

"And I won't be manhandled," she snapped back.

He stepped in front of her, blocking her escape. "You're not moving until you spit out the truth. I've sensed something out of kilter for a long while now, but I didn't want to push you into a discussion you weren't ready for, my woman of mystery." His blue eyes turned fierce, and his voice rose. "If your secrets involve Becky, you'd better start talking before I shake the truth from you."

"Stop it, Jase. Just take a look around you. Everyone's staring," she hissed.

"I don't care if we're onstage at the Met," he shot back. "I don't care if the whole world hears what you have to say."

It was impossible to reason with him. She attempted to jerk her arm free, but his fingers held her immobile, biting into her flesh like the iron teeth of a trap. He knew something serious had happened—he knew it, and yet he refused to allow her the dignity of privacy. If he demanded to hear the truth in front of a room full of onlookers, she'd damn well give it to him.

"Steven Hjortland is Becky's father," she began, foregoing the careful speech she'd planned. Pausing only a moment, she added, "I am her mother."

Her announcement blasted the air. Neither of them moved or spoke for a long moment.

"When Hjortland said . . . I knew then . . ." He shook his head, his anger replaced with raw pain.

Her own fire sputtered out, and her voice was dull as she continued. "I didn't want you to find out this way. I was going to tell you soon." Even to her, that sounded lame.

"Becky's mother," Jase repeated, as though he'd heard nothing else she'd said. He closed his eyes and sucked in a tormented breath. His hand loosened its grip on her arm and fell like a dead thing to his side. "I was a fool not to see it."

"Let's just get out of here. We need to talk this out." She tentatively reached for his hand, but he withdrew as though her touch might be painful and averted his gaze as though he couldn't bear the sight of her. "Try to understand," she said in desperation.

He backed away, still refusing to meet her searching eyes. "Why didn't you tell me?"

"Jase?" she whispered.

Suddenly his eyes were burning into hers again, his face filled with accusation. "How could you live with your lies all this time. I loved . . ." he began but couldn't finish. He turned and walked toward the cafeteria door without looking back.

THE NEXT DAY Steven phoned Reba to say he'd mailed his completed medical form to her, since he was catching a plane that afternoon back to Alaska. It was embarrassing to have to explain what had happened in the cafeteria and apologize for her rude behavior, but somehow she managed to get through it. Steven, instead of being angry as she had expected, was sorry for having ruined things for her. She assured him it wasn't his fault. When he said he'd like to see Becky in person someday, Reba could only tell him that she'd relay his request to Jase. He ended their conversation by wishing her all the best, and Reba heartily returned the sentiment.

For the following ten days Reba waited anxiously for any word from Jase, but when he made no attempt to contact her, hope that he might come around slowly died. She didn't try to phone him, or to see Becky at the stable. The only things that kept her from the depths of depression were her work and the time she'd been spending at The Sunshine Home, helping out Birdie.

"You've got to take some time off," Debbie insisted. She and Reba were at the nurses' station, straightening up the counter during a brief quiet period. Debbie rearranged some charts to make room for a large red poinsettia that had been sent by a grateful patient. "You're running yourself ragged."

Reba bent her head over the computer and suppressed her urge to cry. The tears didn't surprise her. These emotional attacks had overtaken her so often lately that they'd begun to feel like a normal part of life. "He hates me. I'm never going to see him again. I'm never going to see Becky again."

By now Debbie had heard the entire truth. She gave Reba a comforting pat on the back. "He's a louse to treat you this way. Life is so crummy sometimes."

"Especially when you know you've brought your troubles upon yourself."

"Listen, you did what you thought right at the time. Who's Jase Kingsford to judge you?" Enjoying her role as the defender, Debbie's emerald eyes sparkled with indignation. "He wasn't the teenage mother. He didn't have to give up his child. Maybe if he'd spent some time in your shoes, he'd have a little more compassion for you."

Debbie would be pleased to know how reassuring her words were to Reba. She pulled a chart out of the carousel file and made a notation while Debbie went through the routine of checking out a patient. Thank heavens for good friends, Reba mused, wondering how she could have gotten through the past few days alone. When she had told the story of giving up her baby for adoption, Debbie hadn't reacted with the revulsion Reba had expected. When she'd explained why she'd hidden her true identity, Debbie had said she would have done the same. Unlike Jase, Debbie seemed to understand everything.

Debbie bid a cheery goodbye as the departing patient went out the door. She examined the nails of one hand. "I hate these short things we have to wear. I'm putting on nails an inch long for Christmas, and I'm going to stripe them candy-cane red and white. Bob's mom will love that. His parents are throwing a huge engagement bash for us. Bob wants to get married as soon as possible." Debbie's face glowed, and she stared dreamily off into space. "I couldn't believe how much his parents liked me. They said Bob works too hard and that I was just the lively kind of woman he needs. It's a good thing I didn't pretend to be boring, thinking it would please them. Mrs. Burton actually complimented me on that green dress I wore. Could've knocked me over with a feather."

"Are you going there for Christmas?" Reba asked.

"Yeah. What are your plans?"

"After I get off work, I'm going over to my dad's place." Reba returned the chart to the carousel and withdrew another. "Christmas Eve I'm going to Birdie's. I'm helping with the party." When she thought of the Christmas she'd dreamed of spending with Jase and Becky, she couldn't keep her dejection from showing.

"You make me crazy being so miserable," Debbie declared.

"I'll never forget the look on Jase's face...."

"Forget about that. It was the surprise, that's all."

"I guess I could call him," she said uncertainly. "I can't stand much more of this silence." Perhaps it wasn't too late to soothe some of the pain she'd inflicted on the man she so desperately loved. Then if he really meant to end it, she could at least have the satisfaction of knowing she'd made an effort to reach his heart. Honesty. That was a lesson she'd learned the hard way.

She must tell Becky the truth, too. Then for once in her life Reba would harbor no secrets. What was more, she felt Becky had a right to know. She wondered what Jase would think about that. He professed to believe in total honesty, but would his principles hold fast when it came to Becky? He would be terrified of losing her to her mother. She liked the idea of forcing Jase into a gut-wrenching decision.

Before she had time to get cold feet, Reba asked Debbie to cover for her and hurried to the pay phone in the nurses' lounge Thankfully the room was empty. She deposited her coins and dialed his number. When Becky answered, Reba had to force words past the catch in her throat.

"Hi, hon. I need to talk to your dad. Is he there?"

"Yeah, Dad's here. Hey, did you two have a fight?"

Caught off guard, Reba was at a loss. Surely Jase wouldn't have said anything to Becky. "Why?" she proceeded cautiously. "Did he say something like that?"

"He didn't have to. He's been like a bear all week. If he keeps this up, I'm moving out. Can I come live with you?"

"Anytime," she answered, not quite jokingly.

"Just kidding. I'll remember your offer though—just in case." She laughed gaily, then said, "Oh, here's Dad."

There was a pause and the sound of muted conversation. "I'm surprised you have the nerve to call," Jase said in a subzero tone that sent a chill down her spine.

"I want to explain—"

"What?" he interrupted. "Your lies?"

"Just give me a chance," Reba persisted. "Surely a newspaperman would want to hear the entire story. You deserve to know everything... and I deserve the opportunity to tell it to you." She let a weighty pause hang between them. "And Becky deserves to know the truth."

"Not from you."

His stubbornness riled her temper. "Why not from me? How are you going to tell her everything? You aren't her mother! You didn't give her away!"

"Exactly," he lashed back. "I'm the man who raised her for twelve years. I have all the rights where *my daughter* is concerned. You have none."

Reba seethed with mounting rage. "You don't intend to tell her, do you? You're just a hypocrite. You talk truth. You demand complete honesty from everyone else. But you won't take that chance with Becky, will you?"

"You've put me through enough pain already. I've heard all from you I want to hear." With that he hung up.

REBA HURRIED up the steps of her home late the following Friday night, turning her back to the cutting wind that whipped her hair into her face and jamming her key into the frozen lock. She gave the stiff door a heave. As she fell into her living room, she heard the phone ringing and ran into the kitchen, hoping it was Debbie. She needed a long session of "girl talk" to ward off the loneliness that seemed to follow her around these days.

She sank heavily onto a stool when she heard Jase's voice.

"I've done a lot of thinking since we last talked."

"Me, too," she whispered, hands shaking and gripping the counter for support.

"I'll be brief. You were right about Becky needing to hear the facts from you. But I want to be there when you tell her. It's going to be a shock for her."

"Not so much as it was for you," Reba said quietly. "I'll have a chance to start from the beginning. It won't just be dumped on her."

"Yes, well. Is tomorrow too soon? I'd like to finish this business as quickly as possible."

Reba ignored the finality in his voice and concentrated instead on the miracle of receiving another chance. "I'll be there early, before I go to work," she said, and prayed her nerve wouldn't fail her.

IT NEARLY DID. She was in such a frantic state that she missed the freeway exit twice, once getting on and once getting off, before she finally made it to Jase's house a half hour late.

She parked in front of the garage, then reached for her photograph album. Pressing it to her breast, she inhaled deeply to calm herself. No matter how frightened she was, she must pretend to know what she was doing. Jase and Becky wouldn't believe her if she didn't believe in herself. This was her last chance; if she blew it, she'd never see either one of them again.

Reba realized Jase was standing in the front door. His scowl was a jarring contrast to the smiling picture of Santa Claus taped up inside the window next to him. He crossed over to her as she got out of the car.

"Jase, is anything wrong?"

He closed the car door behind her, and they stood facing each other in the weak December sunlight. "Becky knows something's up, and she's waiting for you. I wanted to talk to you before we go inside."

"Okay," she said, her insides rolling with wariness and hope.

"I'm going along with this only because I believe in honesty," he said with grim resignation. Reba's heart sank. Her hope that he'd relented was gone. "I want Becky to know all about you and Steven. However, I don't want you discussing your relationship with me. That's our own private business."

Reba took her time to think this over. It was difficult to string two rational thoughts together when Jase stood so close. He still wanted her; she could feel his desire for her radiating from his taut body, see it smoldering in his eyes. Her heart pounded in reaction. Her blood throbbed. She ached to reach out to him, to use her body to convince him that her love was true. A cerebral as well as a physical man, Jase would respond better to words in this situation. She must convince his mind that she acted out of love.

"I want you to grant me something," Reba said.

He gazed at her suspiciously. "What?"

"That when I'm finished with Becky, you and I go somewhere quiet where we can talk. In light of what we've shared, don't you at least owe me a chance to explain?" Jase pulled back his broad shoulders as though fortifying his defenses against her. He no doubt would prefer to end their relationship without a messy emotional scene, she thought. But his coldness might be only camouflage; he couldn't be so bitter if he didn't still feel strongly for her. When he showed no sign of consenting to her proposal, she took a breath and tossed out the last of her ammunition. "I love you, Jase," she said in an impassioned plea. "You told me you loved me, too. Did you just toss that out during the heat of the moment? Was it only a romantic gesture? It must have been if you'll dismiss me so casually."

His hands flew violently into the air, startling her. His face contorted in impotent anger. "You think this has been easy for me? Lady, I've regretted the day I ever set eyes on you." He turned and began striding toward the house. "Are you coming? Or do I tell her myself?"

Reba had no choice but to follow him inside. Fury, not defeat, filled her breast. If nothing else was accomplished today, she'd find a way to take this arrogant man down a peg.

"Becky's up in her room," Jase said tersely as he crossed to the stairs.

Reba walked slowly behind him. Everywhere festive spirit was in evidence: the humorous sound of Ingrid's Norwegian-accented rendition of "White Christmas" coming from the kitchen, the scent of baking gingerbread filling the air, the sparkling lush silver garlands twined around the mahogany banister. It all seemed to shout to Reba that this was the home of a happy family—a home where she had no right to take part in the singing or baking or decorating.

"Reba!" Becky shouted when they entered her room. She lay sprawled across her bed and patted it to encourage Reba to sit beside her. Although the young girl's expression was puzzled and anxious, joy at seeing her friend again glowed from her eyes. It would take a lot to put a damper on this exuberant soul, Reba thought. "Where have you been?" Becky demanded. "Every day I go to the stables and you're never there."

As Reba sat on the bed, she noticed that on the wall beside them a picture of a teenage movie star had been tacked up among the horse posters. "I haven't been going to the stables lately. How's Amber?"

Becky sat up. "She's wonderful. I've begun to take dressage lessons, and Amber's being trained in that, too. Most of my friends like jumping better, but I think dressage is the *ultimate* skill in horsemanship. That's what I want to compete in."

As Becky continued to chatter about Amber's endless intelligence and ability, Reba listened with only half her attention. Jase's impatient expression told her he wanted this over—and quickly.

Not about to let him intimidate her, she took her time deciding on just the right way to begin what she had to say. She studied the pretty girl sitting across from her. A flowery barrette restrained one side of her unruly hair, and next to her lay a pile of teen magazines. At first Reba was surprised that she wasn't reading a horse book, then noticed again the new picture on the wall. Becky would soon be growing out of her coltish ways and begin exploring fashion and makeup and boys. And she would become even more independent and strong-willed than she was already. Reba could easily imagine Becky being the kind of adventurous teen who finds trouble without even seeking it out. She would need a mother to guide her through those treacherous teen years. Reba wondered if Jase would allow her to play that role.

"You're growing up so fast," Reba mused out loud. "Pretty soon you'll forget about horses altogether."

"Never!" Becky declared.

Reba laughed at her daughter's vehemence. "Well, I'm glad to hear it. I hope you'll always love horses like I do."

"Of course I will," she said solemnly.

Jase moved restlessly, prompting Reba to get on with it. There was no reason to continue putting off the inevitable. Now that Becky seemed more relaxed and receptive, she took a deep breath and began. "I didn't come here today to talk about riding. I have something important to tell you. I don't mean to scare you, but I think you should just hear me out completely before you say anything. Then you can ask all the questions you want, and I'll do my best to answer them."

Becky picked up a stuffed bear and hugged it to her. Her suddenly uneasy gaze flicked from her father, who stood near the window, to Reba. "What's this all about?" she asked neither one in particular.

"It's about you and me," Reba answered.

Reba proceeded to give a detailed account of her early life, telling about her pregnancy, the baby, how hard it had been to give up the child she loved. Becky listened silently as promised, still not knowing she was the child. She stared at the closed album Reba placed in front of her. "Here are some pictures of me at a maternity home—" Reba paused and took a deep breath, "—along with some pictures of you as a baby. Becky, honey, I'm your real mother."

Becky blinked, and the color seemed to drain from her face.

Reba carried on in a voice that was much calmer than she actually felt. "There are only a few photos of you when you were born because your new parents adopted you after just a few days. There's a photo of your natural father, Steven, too. He lives in Alaska now. He said he'd really like to see you someday."

Becky continued to sit stock-still, her eyes fastened on Reba's face. She opened her mouth, but no words came out. Then her chest expanded to draw in a ragged breath, and her gaze lowered to the album. Slowly she lifted the cover. Her wavy blond hair spilled down to hide her face as she studied the first pictures. When she finally lifted her chin to look at Reba, her blue eyes were filled with moisture and disbelief. "Are you really my mother?"

"The only thing I had to give you when you were born was my name, Rebecca Marie."

Becky looked to Jase for confirmation.

"It's true, sweetheart. I didn't know myself until last week."

"I was the one who wrote the letter," Reba continued. "I didn't want to come forward at first because I thought it would be unfair to disrupt your life. Finally I realized that it was just as unfair not to tell you. Despite my good intentions, I made a big mistake keeping my identity a secret for so long. I was afraid that if the truth was known, I wouldn't be able to see you again."

"You thought I'd hate you or something?"

"Not exactly." She slid a pointed glance at Jase. "I was terrified that your father would forbid me to see you. I was afraid he'd think I'd try to take you away from him. I'd never do that, no matter how much I love you." She said again, for emphasis, "I'd never do that."

"If you're really my mother, and you really wanted me, then why didn't you try to find me before?" Becky demanded accusingly.

"When I gave you up for adoption, I relinquished all my rights to see you. Your new parents didn't know who I was, and I didn't know who they were. That's what the agreement was between us. I never intended to go back on my word, even though it was hard to not try to find you when I wanted so much to be with you." Reba went on to tell Becky how she had seen her picture in the paper. "When I saw you at the stable and knew for sure you were my child, it was impossible to resist seeing more of you. The temptation was too great. I'm not that strong a person." Reba paused. She spoke the next words more to herself than to Becky. "It was wrong of me to disturb your life. I made a mess of things."

"Do you wish you'd kept me?"

Reba dropped her gaze to her tightly clenched hands. "I was so scared and confused at the time. I wanted you desperately—but I didn't think I could give you a decent home. Oftentimes I think I made the wrong decision."

"You did want me." Becky's words came out filled with certainty.

"Even though I thought I'd done the right thing by you, I still felt terrible. I thought I must be an awful person to have given away my baby."

"I think you're wonderful," Becky choked out, tears welling. Not the type who cried easily, she hastily wiped her eyes with the back of her arm. But Reba's comforting hand on her knee undid her efforts to hide her emotion. A dam of moisture broke, and she gave herself up to great sobs. When she leaned forward tentatively, Reba opened her arms in welcome. They came together in a hug, both crying now, telling each other how glad they were to be mother and daughter.

When they at last eased apart, Reba noticed that Jase had left the room. "Are you okay?" she asked Becky.

When the girl nodded vigorously in the brave fashion Reba expected, she said, "I know you need to think this over. Keep the album. I have to talk to your father, and then I might be leaving. If I don't come back and say goodbye, will that be all right?"

"Dad's been real mad at you," Becky admitted. "He hasn't said anything, but I know, because whenever I mentioned you, he'd change the subject right away."

"I know. He's as confused about this as you and I are."

"Is everything going to be okay?"

Reba bit down on her bottom lip. No more lies, she told herself. "I don't know, honey. I hope so."

Leaving Becky, knowing that she might never see her again, was one of the hardest things Reba had ever had to do. She stood to go, refusing to cry again, instead bestowing a brilliant smile on her daughter. Then, not trusting herself to speak, she quickly departed.

She walked down the wide hallways of Jase's grand house, feeling very small and fragile and overwhelmed by all that had happened. At this point she couldn't imagine what the future held, what type of relationship she and Becky and Jase might have. Her heart knew that Becky had accepted her without reservations. As for Jase, she didn't know. All she could do was try again to reach him, and she didn't intend to leave this house until she'd done just that.

She found him in his study, in front of the window looking out. In the semidarkness of the room the light outside defined his tall, athletic physique. He didn't turn around when she softly called his name.

"All right," she began with more boldness than her quivering heart felt. "If you want to pout like a spoiled five-year-old, you go right ahead. That's not going to stop me from having my say."

He turned, his gaze assessing her. "There's only one thing I'm interested in hearing from you."

"And what's that?"

"Your promise that you'll never go near the stable again, that you won't come within ten miles of my daughter."

Reba squeezed her eyes shut as she took a breath. "I was hoping you wouldn't do that. I know I have no rights where she's concerned, but I was counting on some compassion."

"I'm not worried about your feelings, Reba. All I want is to have Becky's and my life back to normal. If that's even possible."

"I see," she murmured.

"If I even suspect you're sneaking around to visit her, I'll get a restraining order."

He was speaking to her as though she were a dangerous stranger, someone to be feared. She folded her shaking hands across her breasts. "I give you my word that I won't see or talk to Becky again unless you give me permission."

"Well, you're not going to get it. And just remember, I'll be keeping a close eye on her. I've lost all trust in you."

Reba ignored the stabbing pains his words inflicted, instead seeking a way to destroy his infuriating self-control. "I can't say I'm not hurt and disappointed. Especially since you are just doing this to get back at me for hurting you."

"This hasn't got anything to do with you and me. The two issues are separate," he declared, a trace of anger now in his voice. "I wouldn't use Becky that way. I don't play emotional games. Don't accuse me of your unethical tricks."

Reba couldn't stand still any longer. She began to pace, throwing her arms out as she demanded, "What would you have had me do? Tell you right from the beginning who I was? I thought it best to keep the past in the past. No need to stir up trouble. And then . . . and then I fell in love with you. Can't you see what a terrible position that placed me in?" She stepped closer to him, right up into his face. "I planned to tell you. I thought if I waited until I was certain you loved me, too, that I might have a chance." She looked at him directly, entreating him with her wet eyes. "I thought if you loved me enough, your stupid principles wouldn't matter anymore." He stood motionless, his face an unforgiving granite mask. When tears began to burn her eyes, she wanted to hide her face, but forced herself to remain steadfast. *Let him see the misery he's caused*, she thought bitterly. "I was wrong. All you care about is your principles. 'Truth Above All,'" she quoted, adding, "and principles above people."

"At least I *have* a moral conscience," he hurled back. "Get out of here. I don't want to look at your lying face for one more minute."

She stepped back, about to run from the room, when his hands shot out to haul her to him. He wrapped his arms around her, holding her body still while he crushed her lips beneath his. It wasn't a loving embrace; it seemed as though he were trying to purge her from his system. The embrace was as cruel as it was erotic. Reba felt a hot and terrible ache of desire as the kiss deepened. At that charged moment Jase could have pulled her to the floor and ripped off her clothes, and she would have urged him on. The time for words had passed; now she was willing to break through his defenses any way she could.

"Make love to me," she whispered when he released her bruised lips. "I want you so."

"Oh, Reba, why do you torture me?" His breaths came in great rasping gulps as he strained to leash his body. "You broke my trust . . . my heart."

"I broke nothing! You're doing this to yourself. I love you! And I know you want me."

Just when she sensed his armor cracking, he regained control and withdrew his arms from her. "No. I only want you to go," he said softly.

AS SOON AS SHE GOT OFF work on December twenty-fourth, Reba hurried to The Sunshine Home. She went straight to the kitchen and by seven o'clock had several dozen cookies to show for her efforts. Birdie, her ample bosom covered by a practical red apron, bustled over to the counter where Reba had just produced a sheetful of little wreaths with the cookie press.

"Oh, you're so talented, Reba," Birdie fussed. "Just look at those pretty things with their red candy bows and green sparkle. As soon as the girls finish decorating the tree, I want you to teach them how to make those."

"Glad to." Reba couldn't help but glow like a praise-starved fifteen-year-old at Birdie's comment. She had known it would brighten her spirits to be around Birdie and to concentrate on doing something for others. When she was alone, all she could thing of was the finality of her parting from Jase.

"It's wonderful having you with us," Birdie went on as she popped the cookie sheet into the oven. "It helps, you know, for the girls to see one of our own graduates doing so well. I hope you can spend more time here."

"I'm afraid I might be leaving Seattle. I've been thinking about applying for a job in Portland."

Undaunted by Reba's depression, Birdie smiled cheerfully. "Oh, my dear, I wouldn't be in such a rush if I were you."

"Jase is adamant, Birdie. He doesn't trust me, and I think he'd shoot me on sight if I went near Becky. I can't live like this." She wiped her hands on a dish towel, thinking about the bridle she'd mailed Becky for Christmas and wondering if Jase would return the gift with a nasty note telling her to stay out of their lives. "It's an impossible situation. What if Jase or Becky and I happened to see each other in a mall or something? It would be awful. I think my heart would break all over again. My presence in Seattle will only make it harder for everyone concerned."

"Mr. Kingsford needs some time to adjust. After all, you gave him quite a shock," Birdie said, turning her back to Reba as she glazed a ham for dinner. "He told me about it, you know."

Reba stopped what she was doing to stare at the plump little woman. "When did you talk to him?"

"Oh, the other day. I called him to see how Becky was doing. He didn't seem like such a hard man."

"Huh! A boulder would be more flexible. I couldn't get through to him, no matter how I tried. If only I'd confessed before Jase found me out. He thinks the worst of me now. Sometimes I think the worst of myself."

Even though Christmas that year was miserable for Reba, it was a festive time for the youthful residents of The Sunshine Home. Everyone agreed that the tree was beautiful, the dinner delicious, and the cookies Reba had taught them to bake as good to eat as they were to look at.

"It's hard to believe it's Christmas Eve already," Birdie said as she settled in the window chair across from Reba. Outside, the world was dark and still. But inside, the room blazed with light and fairly vibrated with the enthusiasm of a dozen teenage girls. She surveyed her bright-eyed lot, looking as excited as a child herself. "Aren't they having a grand time? They're all still children, you know. Just like you were when you were here. Children having children." She cocked her head, the little topknot bobbing to one side. "It's fun to put some magic back in their lives. They have to grow up so fast. Just for Christmas they can be young again— I see to that." She glanced back over her shoulder, out the window. "Oh, good! My surprise has arrived. How the girls will love this! And I think this will bring some magic to your life, too, my dear." Birdie's little dark eyes sparkled as she bent her head and whispered conspiratorially to Reba, "Go open the back door, will you?"

Wondering what had Birdie so keyed up, Reba wended her way through the chaos in the living room and headed for the rear of the big house. There she opened the door to white falling snow, a red-suited Santa and a bright green elf.

"Merry Christmas, Reba!" cried the elf, throwing out her arms and giving Reba a wild hug. Becky, her long blond curls bouncing under a little feathered cap, grinned up at her with cheeks flushed from excitement. "Oh, I can't wait to tell you—"

"Becky, hush." Jase's deep voice sent thrills up Reba's spine. "You know what we talked about."

Her heart pounding, Reba slowly raised her gaze from Becky to the face of the tall Santa. There was no mistaking those ocean-blue eyes. But the expression in them was so different from what she had last seen. Even in the dim back-porch lighting, she could discern a twinkle.

"Jase," she blurted out his name in astonishment. "What on earth?"

Becky bounced in front of her, grabbing Reba's hands and spinning her around with a twelve-year-old's bountiful energy. "Isn't this super? Dad and I talked about—"

"Becky," Jase warned.

"You and everything. Oh, Reba, everything really is going to be okay. I've wanted to see you before, but Dad wouldn't let me. It's so hard to believe that you really are my mother, but I'm glad that it's true." Her flow of words halted abruptly, then she asked shyly, "Do I keep calling you Reba now?"

"If you'd like to."

"Yes. I would." When she opened her mouth to speak again, Jase quickly stepped forward and placed a restraining hand across her lips.

"If I can get a word in here," he said, chuckling. "I was going to call you before, but Birdie told me you'd be here today and I thought it would be nice to surprise you. No, that's not completely true. I wanted to talk to you desperately! I almost called you yesterday, but Becky convinced me to wait until today."

Becky, still a silent captive of her father, nodded confirmation.

"I'm very surprised," Reba said softly.

Jase looked deeply into her dark brown eyes, filled with such love and suffering that he could barely keep himself from taking her into his arms then and there. It had been her eyes that had first captivated him. So large and expressive, they revealed her true feelings now, just as they always had. Her eyes had never been able to keep secrets.

He'd been such a fool! During the past weeks he'd done some hard thinking and had come to realize that she hadn't lied to him with any malicious intent. She had done what she truly thought was best for all concerned. And she had always acted out of love.

Becky managed to wiggle out of her father's clutches. "We've been so busy, getting these costumes. And look at all these gifts we bought!" She spun back to Jase and patted the fat white bag slung over his shoulder.

At the sound of heel taps on the linoleum, Reba turned to see Birdie hurrying toward them, looking quite pleased with herself and calling out, "Hello, Mr. Kingsford—I mean Santa. I'm so thrilled you came today." She patted Becky's shoulder, smiling down at the young girl. "This elf must be Becky. You can call me Birdie. Why don't you come with me? We're going to sing carols around the piano. A little later we'll bring in Santa and open presents. Right now I think Santa and Reba have some talking to do."

Becky looked over her shoulder and gave her father a conspiratorial wink so obvious that everyone laughed. When they were gone, Jase lowered his bundle to the floor and moved toward her. "Your mouth is still hanging open."

"It's entitled to. What's the meaning of all this?"

"Birdie asked me to play Santa this year." He rubbed his forehead and grimaced. "Good God, Reba. I had to see you again. These last two weeks have been hell. I couldn't leave things the way they were between us."

"I can't apologize anymore," she bit out. "There's nothing new I can add to what I've already said. I've hurt you and broken your trust in me.... That's all there is to it." Reba averted her gaze to her hands. "I'm planning to move away. I thought you'd like to know that I won't be around to cause you any more trouble."

"You've certainly done your share of that," he said soberly. "But Becky won't give you up." He paused. "And neither will I." Suddenly he tore off the white beard and flung it aside, moving toward her at the same time. Without another word he pulled her to him. "I can't stay away from you," he breathed, his mustache traveling across her cheek to entice her skin with the silky roughness she adored.

With her body crying out for him, it was hard to remember how deep their problems were. "But, Jase, what about trust? You said you'd never be able to trust me again."

"I said a lot of stupid things. They don't matter now. All that matters is that I love you and you love me."

She felt his arms, hard and strong around her, the heat of his desire burning against her as he whispered, "From that first night when I trapped a sweet wild gypsy in my bed, I knew I had to have you forever in my life."

Reba clamped down on the joy spreading through her. Nothing was resolved between them; she couldn't stand being disappointed again. "I kept the truth from you. Even though I know now that keeping my past a secret was wrong, it doesn't change things for us." She must bring the issue out in the open; if they didn't trust each other, nothing else could really work for them. "I began our relationship with a lie."

"It's unimportant how our relationship began or at what point in time you fell in love with me. I know you love me now, and that's all that counts."

His words intoxicated her, and she yearned to lose herself in them. But she had to pursue the underlying conflict. "Yes, love is all that counts. *I* believe that." She tilted her head back so that she could look directly into his face. "But do *you* . . . really? Won't your principles always come between us?"

"Principles be damned! I almost lost you because I couldn't bend them. I can't swear that I'll always be flexible, but you've taught me to see fallible human beings in a more compassionate light. I've had a lot of time to think about what you told Becky about your life. I understand how hard it must have been for you to open up after all these years. I wonder now if I wouldn't have proceeded in exactly the same manner if I had been you. Yes, you lied. But I understand why you did, and I believe you had the best of intentions."

"And do you believe I really planned on telling you who I am, the whole truth?"

He stroked her hair. "If you say it's true, then I'll take you at your word. What's more, I'll never doubt you again."

"Oh, Jase," Reba cried, at last allowing herself to believe that her most cherished fantasy had become a reality. "Do you mean that?"

His mouth began to curve at the edges. "The simple truth is that I love you."

Strains of "Silent Night" floated through the air. They continued to hold each other close, as though fearing any new separation, until Becky arrived to say it was time to open presents.

"Did you ask her, Dad?"

He silenced his daughter this time with a ferocious glower. "One more word . . ."

"Okay, okay! I won't bug you again." She grinned at Reba. "I'm so happy."

Reba removed herself from Jase's arms so that she could give Becky a hug. "So am I. Incredibly so."

They followed Jase into the living room where he deposited the presents under the tree with instructions for Becky to hand them out. After some obligatory "Ho, ho, hos," he took Reba's hand and led her into a dimly lit corner.

"You're sure you're not just getting carried away with Christmas sentiment?" Reba asked him, her old doubts still not completely quelled. That Jase might actually love her and want her to be a part of his and Becky's life seemed too good to be true. Any minute now she would wake up from this glorious dream. The carolers finished their song and made a headlong dash to the eight-foot blue spruce that dominated the center of the room. "It's a crazy season," she said. "How do I know this new attitude of yours is going to last throughout the new year?"

"You just have to trust me." He gave her a teasing wink.

They watched, grinning, as the girls attacked the gifts. Squeals of delight pierced the air and bright wrapping paper flew everywhere.

"I almost forgot," Jase said. "I have a little Christmas present here for you. Perhaps this will convince you my love is true."

He dug into the pocket of his red velvet Santa coat and pulled out an elegant silver-wrapped box. She opened it with trembling fingers. The largest, most brilliant pear-shaped diamond she had ever seen rested inside.

For a full minute she remained speechless. "It's...it's a diamond ring."

"Does that mean yes?"

She held out her left hand, her trembling fingers spread wide for him to slip on the symbol of his love. Her tears magnified the facets of the stone, splaying a pattern of light rays that completely filled her view. Love for Jase filled her heart to the brim, leaving no more room for doubt. She raised her blurry gaze to the blue eyes that so clearly revealed his feelings. "I have nothing for you," she murmured. "I had no way of knowing."

Becky strolled by and caught her Dad's eye. When he grinned and nodded, she let out a cheer. The girls gathered around the piano again. Birdie began to play, and Becky ran over to join them, ringing bells in accompaniment, as the girls sang a joyous round of "Deck the Halls with Boughs of Holly."

Tenderly Jase brushed the curly, dark wisps from Reba's forehead. "You've already given me the finest gift I could ever receive. Your love." He bent to kiss Reba deeply. "And that's the honest truth."

Harlequin Temptation

COMING NEXT MONTH

#233 MURPHY'S LAW JoAnn Ross

Hannah Greene had hoped for a fresh start in New Chance, Arizona, but trouble seemed to have followed her from Connecticut. It was only when Trace Murphy came to her rescue that she dared hope her luck was changing....

#234 GYPSY Glenda Sanders

Anna Maria had left her Gypsy roots behind, but not her passionate Gypsy nature. And it didn't take much for Sheriff Thomas Banning to stir up both....

#235 MONKEY BUSINESS Cassie Miles

Anthropologist Erica Swanson didn't want anything to interfere with the adventures she had planned for her future. But that was before she met Nick Barron...and envisioned even more exciting exploits in the here and now.

#236 A WINNING BATTLE Carla Neggers

Christopher O. Battle, a nationally syndicated columnist, resisted the urge to lampoon a professional organizer, namely Page B. Harrington. In exchange, *she* managed to resist uncluttering his apartment. Falling in love, however, was something neither one had any control over.

Harlequin Temptation dares to be different!

Once in a while, we Temptation editors spot a romance that's truly innovative. To make sure *you* don't miss any one of these outstanding selections, we'll mark them for you.

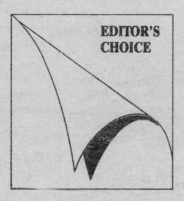

EDITOR'S CHOICE

When the ''Editors' Choice'' fold-back appears on a Temptation cover, you'll know we've found that extra-special page-turner!

THE

Temptation

EDITORS